"I detest you," Erica said sharply.

Her face was flushed, her breasts rising and falling sharply.

"Perhaps," Rafe conceded, the twist of triumph on his lips proof that he was well aware of the effort of will it had taken for her not to capitulate to his kiss. "But whether you're in love with Caddis or not, there's something between us, Erica, that even you can't deny...something that's always been there. They say physical compatibility isn't everything in a relationship, but it is certainly a very important part."

So he thought she was in love with the other man. Well, let him think it! "I wouldn't know."

A dark eyebrow lifted. "Are you trying to tell me you're still as innocent as that pleading seventeen-year-old I couldn't be a heel enough to give in to?"

ELIZABETH POWER was once a legal secretary, but when the compulsion to write became too strong, she abandoned affidavits, wills and conveyances in favor of a literary career. Her husband, she says, is her best critic. And he's a good cook, too—often readily taking over the preparation of meals when her writing is in full flow. They live in a three-hundred-year-old English country estate cottage, surrounded by woodlands and wildlife. Who wouldn't be inspired to write?

Books by Elizabeth Power

HARLEQUIN PRESENTS
1078—SHADOW IN THE SUN
1341—THE DEVIL'S EDEN

HARLEQUIN ROMANCE
2825—RUDE AWAKENING

Don't miss any of our special offers. Write to us at the following address for information on our newest releases.

Harlequin Reader Service
P.O. Box 1397, Buffalo, NY 14240
Canadian address: P.O. Box 603,
Fort Erie, Ont. L2A 5X3

ELIZABETH POWER

seed of vengeance

Harlequin Books

TORONTO • NEW YORK • LONDON
AMSTERDAM • PARIS • SYDNEY • HAMBURG
STOCKHOLM • ATHENS • TOKYO • MILAN

Harlequin Presents first edition March 1992
ISBN 0-373-11445-1

Original hardcover edition published in 1990
by Mills & Boon Limited

SEED OF VENGEANCE

CHAPTER ONE

ERICA didn't know how much longer she could bear it, watching her father being treated like a criminal.

Now that the afternoon session was in progress, he was sitting, hands clasped tensely on the table he shared with his defence counsel, that shock of white hair and the gaunt lines of his face making him look more like an old man, Erica thought sadly, instead of the leading force behind Witney Laboratories. So much for English justice. Dear God! Could his heart stand it?

Unable to help herself, unobtrusively, she slipped out of the stuffy courtroom, welcoming the cooler air in the lobby. Beyond the windows, London throbbed and roared and hooted, lights cutting through the murk, prompting a glance towards her slim wrist. Hardly half-past three, and already it was getting dark!

'Erica.' The voice that spoke her name seemed to freeze her, cold as a statue, blood draining from her face, back stiffening beneath a creamy white coat.

Rafe Cameron! He must have been in court, and she hadn't noticed him, she realised, turning stiffly then, her throat contracting, bitter memory paling against the stark reality.

He was all she remembered and more, from his splendid height and that self-assured way he held his dark head, to those strong features moulded with hard arrogance—that striking authority in that determined jaw and cheekbones, in the sensual, yet uncompromising mouth. But that raw, animal vitality—the impact of that sheer masculine presence—she had forgotten, feeling it now with her stomach muscles knotting as she watched him stride confidently towards her.

'What are *you* doing here?' Somehow she managed to conceal the tremor in her voice, her shock at seeing him—though her pulse was racing—refusing to allow her emotions to reflect themselves in her face.

'It's a public hearing,' he reminded her with the barest of shrugs, the expensive cut of a dark business suit unable to disguise the superb physical power of him beneath. 'Being accused of stealing the formula for a new miracle migraine drug doesn't exactly get confined to the back pages of the tabloids,' that deep, velvety voice assured her, its tone, richly enhanced, she was reminded all too acutely, by that barest suggestion of Scots. 'Particularly when one drug company's suing another's MD personally for the crime—and more particularly when the accused is the eminent Sir Joshua Witney.' A thick eyebrow arched—like his hair, as black as Satan—the small gesture so painfully familiar to her that she had to look away, unable for a moment to meet the chilling clarity of his eyes, scared, too, of revealing just how unsettled she was at seeing him again.

'What's wrong, Erica?' Those eyes, cold as sapphires, raked over her small, tense features, taking in the arresting combination of brown eyes and blonde, shoulder-length hair, the gentle forehead, high cheekbones and the straight, patrician nose that unjustly lent her an air of almost haughty beauty; and that strong, male mouth hardened. 'Afraid you'll never be able to look down that lovely nose at anyone again? Well I'm sure you'll manage it—somehow.' That velvet voice was condemning, making her shudder. 'It does seem rather ironic, though, doesn't it, Erica, that *your* father should be accused of stealing...?'

He didn't finish, but his meaning was clear enough. Hadn't he accused her of thinking herself too good for him five years ago? That it would be demeaning to her—a girl born to wealth and position—to marry the son of a man who was merely in her father's employ?

Her lashes came down to conceal the pain that thinking back rekindled, because he had made her pay for that—and in the cruellest way, her small, twisted smile directed at herself, because, of course, he hadn't known how desperately she had loved him. But whatever he had thought of her father's wealth then, he could probably match it now, she suspected, because he had done well for himself—and through sheer hard work, that tenacity and gut determination leading him from irrigation engineer into a management take-over some years back that had put him among the princes of industry while still only thirty-two.

The sheer ruthlessness such achievement demanded sent a little shiver through her, but, squaring her shoulders, refusing to let him undermine her composure, she said calmly, 'My father didn't steal that formula, even if Burketts are saying he did. It's an unfortunate coincidence they launched their new drug the same month we launched MG3, but that's all it is—coincidence. Dad would never do anything underhand or illegal—a man knighted for his services to industry, for heaven's sake! He's a man of honour, integrity—everyone knows that, although I'd hardly expect *you* to understand what that means!'

She couldn't help flinging it at him, her mind's picture of him in another woman's arms after he had already proposed to her surprisingly still able to hurt with an acuteness she was far from happy to acknowledge. Fleetingly, pain revealed itself with the contempt in her challenging features, brown eyes clashing with icy blue when he took a step nearer, awakening her startled senses to the disturbing power of his masculinity. She could *feel* his angry warmth, smell the subtle fragrance of his cologne, the reckless memory of that hard, passionate mouth on hers making her step back almost too guardedly, her colour flaring, ashamed to realise an attraction that even his brutal disloyalty of five years ago hadn't nullified.

That cruel mouth quirked, those cool eyes—like that brilliant brain—disconcertingly aware. But, ignoring her taunt, he said only, 'Oh, I've no doubt of your father's innocence. Or of his claims that formula MG3 was originally my father's baby and therefore discovered at Witneys—even if the company did decide to sit on it for the next five years.'

'Then...you believe it?' she murmured incredulously, because it was the thing Sir Joshua had been stressing all along. Rafe's father, Adam, had worked in research at Witneys and, as a respected colleague of Sir Joshua—himself a scientist—had liaised closely with him over new breakthroughs, formula MG3 being no exception. But as Rafe had said, the company had shelved his father's findings, thinking them too new and experimental, until recently, when Sir Joshua had revived a personal interest in them himself.

'What I believe hardly matters, does it?' he stated, as condescendingly as if he were talking to a child, the deep, indifferent syllables seeming to echo chillingly around the stark walls. 'It isn't me he has to convince, is it? And that witness the opposition produced was pretty persuasive.'

She felt his cold regard tug across her face, probing, searching for some flicker of weakness, the fear that made her tremble—not only for her father but from this daunting meeting with Rafe—though she concealed it well, even as she accepted that he was right.

The witness had said he'd been offered money by Sir Joshua originally to get hold of certain research notes on the new drug from his rivals' premises, though he said he'd refused. But the man was an ex-employee of Witneys, dismissed, some months back, for misconduct, and it was apparent to Erica that he still bore a grudge. The problem was, though, that a laboratory fire at Witneys recently, which had reached the Records Office, had destroyed a great number of important files, including those of the initial discovery of MG3, so that only rough, undated data existed concerning it now. And Adam Cameron, of course, had already been dead for some years...

'Surely...' Realising, breathlessly, she looked up into that strong, unyielding countenance—hers suddenly hopeful, assessing. That hard sophistication and poise, that intellect, and that indisputable influence he had these days... Just one word from him could sway a court's decision. 'Surely, your father must have said something to *you* about his discovery... been excited about it...' Her voice tailed off, but the plea was unmistakable, and she despised herself for it when she saw the glint of satisfaction in Rafe's eyes.

'My father seldom talked about his work.' The deep tones were cold—dispassionate. 'And even if I could help your father, just give me one good reason why I should?'

The flaying contempt in that last remark made her flinch, and she dropped her gaze, bitterly reminded of what little regard he had had for Sir Joshua before—as his actions had proved.

'Well, why not for old times' sake, Rafe?' she murmured with a frosty smile, tilting her small chin to his, determined not to let him see the anguish it was causing her having to stand here and face him like this. And with added poignancy, 'Or does a man in your position require some sort of fee for his time these days?'

He didn't answer immediately, as a young bewigged advocate was passing, black gown flying out behind him as he hurried by. Then a door closed, a cold, hollow sound, and they were alone again.

'Are you trying to bribe me, Erica?' For a moment, that dark sorcery she'd fallen prey to as a teenager broke through the cynical smile, tinging the soft words with sensuality. She swallowed, feeling that blue gaze moving over her with a lazy insolence, seeming to burn where it lingered, as if he were remembering how she had felt beneath his hands—her eager response. Cruel memory sent wings of colour across her pale cheeks, so that something curved his lips again, cool and discerning. 'What precisely did you have in mind?'

Her flush deepening, she saw the hard derision in his eyes. He had wanted to humiliate her, she realised, hating him, herself—for giving him the opportunity to do so. But, pulling her face into more controlled lines, she breathed with scathing emphasis, 'Quite seriously, I wouldn't ask your help if my life depended on it!'

'No?' The intimidation in that one word, in the arching scepticism of an eyebrow sent a cold shiver down her spine. She started to say something, but was cut short as doors suddenly opened and people spilled out—counsellors, members of the public and the media—while outside in the street she could see TV crews and reporters hovering, waiting to pounce like a pack of starving wolves the moment Sir Joshua showed his face.

'Don't worry—they'll have a field day.' The deep, cynical voice lanced through her with cruel penetration, that shrewd gaze having followed hers to the chilling scene outside. 'I can only wish him luck,' he said perfunctorily, thrusting a hand into his trouser pocket, 'because, by heaven, before they're through with him, he's going to need it!'

He swung away from her then, a noticeable, masculine figure shouldering his way through the crowd, leaving Erica staring after him with tears of wounded anger stinging her eyes.

Why had he come here? Simply to gloat over her father's misfortune? To see her unhappy? How could he? How could he still want to hurt her? she wondered, bitterly, despising herself for the dart of pain that shot through her. After all, he meant nothing to her now. *Nothing!* she assured herself with unjustified vehemence. So why had she let him unsettle her as he had?

She started as someone caught her arm, turning to face the more amiable features of Graham Caddis.

'I was just coming out to see where you were before they decided to adjourn things—yet again,' he told her, sounding exasperated. And with a glance over Erica's shoulder, 'Wasn't that Rafe Cameron you were talking to?' He knew who Rafe was. Who didn't? she thought, in unwilling appreciation of the man's rapier-sharp brain and driving energies. His enterprises these days made headline news!

She nodded, moving so that Graham wouldn't see the turmoil in her proud yet fragile features, wishing she could have stayed in the office.

'What did he want?'

She exhaled a small sigh, watching him rake back a recalcitrant strand of brown hair.

Slightly built and with that ex-public-school look about him, at twenty-four—two years older than herself—Graham was Witneys' most promising executive, as well as a good friend. But he had only been with the company a year and didn't know of her past involvement with Rafe, and at that moment she didn't even want to talk about the man.

'He was in court and happened to mention the case,' she answered evasively, moving, in an anxious effort to reach Sir Joshua before he stepped through the open, external doors into the merciless claws of the Press.

'Things didn't look too rosy in there.' She heard Graham's heart-sinking comment at her shoulder as she pushed her way through the crowd. 'This case is really taking its toll of your father's health and his counsel thinks it could drag on with him on bail like this for months. In all seriousness, I'm wondering how much more he's going to be able to stand with that weak heart of his.'

Wasn't that exactly what she had been wondering earlier? Just looking at her father made her stomach muscles clench sickeningly. He looked drawn—positively ill.

'Is it true that you first learned about Burketts' plans for this new drug during a meal at the Burketts' house, sir?'

'What do you think this is likely to do to Witney shares?'

'Do you have any comments to make at all?'

Questions came thick and fast as they stepped out into the cold February afternoon, people rushing forward, cameras flashing endlessly as the three of them climbed into the waiting Rolls. Then mercifully the car was speeding away.

'Shall I come back to the house with you, Dad?' Erica viewed him anxiously as he finished issuing instructions to his chauffeur and slumped tiredly back against the rear seat.

'No,' he declined, his breathing shallow. 'I'm only popping in to pick up a suitcase. I'm taking a break. Doctor's orders,' he conveyed to her with a weary smile. 'I'm going to spend a few days at the cottage.'

Silently, Erica had to accept that a few days in their quiet Yorkshire retreat wouldn't do him any harm at all. He hadn't made any reference to seeing Rafe Cameron in court, though, and she exhaled an inaudible sigh of relief, relaxing a little. He'd been disappointed when she'd broken up with Rafe, and she'd never told him why. Now with a determined tightening of her lips she made a conscious effort to put the man out of her mind.

'Are you sure you'll be all right?' she asked, worried about him, placing a caring hand on his arm. She was extremely close to her father, and always had been, her mother having died before she was old enough even to remember her.

'Yes, yes,' he reassured her, 'but I'm not so convinced about you.' Concerned blue eyes took in her pale features, her gracefully slim figure beneath the white coat. 'This wretched affair is robbing you of your appetite, and you didn't have anything at all at lunchtime. Could you take her somewhere, Graham, and see that she gets something to eat?' And with a wry smile at Erica, 'I can't have my favourite marketing manager going down with anorexia, now, can I?'

'It'll be a pleasure, sir,' she heard Graham responding swiftly—eagerly—and knew she'd have to comply with her father's wishes, though at that moment eating was the last thing she felt like doing.

'You know, he's proud of you,' Graham told her twenty minutes later, when they were sitting in her favourite Indian restaurant. 'I know he's helped you a lot, but he wasn't the one who swotted for that degree in marketing, and it isn't his flair that's put that touch of poignancy into our advertising. You're a real asset to his company, Erica, and he knows it. I just wish he'd recognise some potential in me and put me out of my suspense over that promotion.'

Swallowing some mineral water, as her curry was very hot, Erica smiled understandingly. Poor Graham, she thought. His promotion meant everything to him. But at the moment Sir Joshua had more pressing things on his mind.

As for herself, she mused, pushing her fork into some fluffy white rice, if Graham though she was successful in her job, it was because she had allowed little else into her life since that bitter experience with Rafe.

She didn't want to think about him, but the thoughts came crowding back, dragging her mind unwillingly across the years.

She'd met him first at a dinner party she'd attended with her father at Adam Cameron's house, and, young and impressionable as she'd been, Rafe's attraction for her had been instant and overpowering. There had been other parties after that, and always when they had met he had treated her with the gentle, amused indulgence with which one treated a child—until the night of her father's barbecue.

She'd been arguing with one of the company chemists against live animal experiments in medical research, and at some point Rafe had come along and joined their small group. He hadn't said a great deal, watching her with a brooding male interest that had both scared and excited her, so that, unable to cope with the sensations he was evoking in her, she had wandered inside under the pretext of getting a jacket. A moth had been fluttering hopelessly between the window-pane and the curtains—lured in by the light—and, standing on tiptoe, she had cupped her hands carefully around it, trying to coax it back through the open window, until it had flitted out of her grasp. Then sure, stronger hands had reached over her head, gently catching the little insect—releasing it into the night—and she had turned to see Rafe smiling down at her in a way that had made her pulse throb.

'St Francis really had nothing on you, did he?' he had said softly, and then he had bent and kissed her—gently at first, then with a hard, demanding passion that had given life to hers, awakening her sexuality and her love for him with an intensity that had only grown and

deepened during that long, hot summer. He'd made her
laugh as no one else had ever done, teaching her things
about life that she had learned eagerly from the benefit
of his ten years' advantage over her. Seventeen, and fresh
out of college, she had lived only for the hours she could
spend in his company, walking with him under balmy,
starlit skies, exchanging secrets, drowning in the un-
equalled ecstasy of his lovemaking. She'd never been able
to have enough of him, or he of her, as far as his immense self-control would allow, because he had never
actually crossed that final threshold to make her fully
his, even when she—driven delirious from his kisses—
had begged him to, innocently offering him the gift of
her untutored body; and she'd believed it was out of
respect for her youth that he'd exercised that admirable
self-discipline. She'd been happier than she'd ever been
in her life, until the day he'd starting talking about marriage, and then she had retreated into her shell.

He'd said he'd wanted children, lots of children—she
recalled those words like drops of molten lead searing
through her heart—and, though he'd spoken with teasing
exaggeration, she had realised just how much having an
heir would mean to him—and exactly how he would react
if she told him the truth. That because of internal
problems—an operation for cystic fallopian tubes and
the removal of a diseased ovary the year before—she
was left as only half a woman, told by the doctors that
her chances of becoming pregnant were very, very slim.
So she had kept it to herself, not knowing what to do
when Rafe had proposed, wanting more than anything
in the world to pretend that the cruel results of that operation didn't exist, and to simply accept, but she
couldn't be as deceitful and unfair to him as that. So
she had told him she'd think about it, evading the issue
when he started putting pressure on her to give him an
answer, hurting unbearably when he became impatient

and irritable with her when she wouldn't, never dreaming he'd find his consolation with Laverne...

Involuntarily she shivered, picking at the meal she had suddenly lost all appetite for, remembering the agony of his betrayal. The day after she'd found out, she'd begged a surprised Sir Joshua to let her go to Switzerland to study—desperate as she had been to conceal her pain from everyone—to get away. So he had complied, and she had worked hard, putting all her energies into her career, determined not to get involved with anyone emotionally again for a long time. And, absorbed solely with her work, she had thought herself reasonably happy, that the old scars had healed—until today, when Rafe had suddenly made a reappearance outside that court...

He was still plaguing her thoughts when she left the office that evening with Graham, although fortunately he didn't seem to notice that unusual reticence about her.

'Going straight home?' he queried, watching her unlock the red Mercedes coupé in the company car park. 'Would you by any chance fancy some company later?' He shot her a look of such wry expectancy over the turned-up collar of his overcoat that she had to smile.

'Thanks, but not tonight,' she demurred, pulling her own coat more closely around her shoulders as there was a nip in the air. 'I've got rather a lot of work to catch up on,' she explained regretfully. There was an export package to market that she needed to give some thought to, as well as the artwork for some posters for an exhibition later in the month. 'Thanks for your support today. I know Dad was glad to see a sympathetic face in court.' Leaning across, she gave him a friendly peck on the cheek. 'Perhaps some other time...'

She could see he was disappointed, but he took the brush-off amicably enough—probably because he was used to it by now, she thought feelingly as she drove away. They got on well, and she had grown very fond of him during the past few months that they had been going out together, but, even so, she still couldn't bring herself to allow Graham—or any man for that matter—into the very vulnerable area of her heart, to get too close to her. She had been bruised too deeply the first time...

Half an hour later she was tripping up the steps to her flat. It was a ground-floor flat in a Georgian house, set in a little square of similar houses, the tiny private park in the middle bleak and dark now, making her shiver as she opened her front door, grateful for the light switch just inside.

Then suddenly she froze, tried to scream and couldn't—paralysed with fear from the hand clamped over her mouth, the ironlike strength of the arm around her midriff.

'Don't make a scene...I'm not going to hurt you.' Somehow that deep, masculine voice registered on her terrified ears. Rafe Cameron! 'Let's go inside, shall we? I've always been averse to discussing anything on the doorstep—particularly a woman's.'

The solid warmth of his body burned into her as he half carried, half pushed her through the door, but once inside he let her go, and she swung round, hair flying wildly, her brown eyes widening in anger.

'What the hell do you want?' Her throat contracted painfully as she saw him closing the front door. 'What do you think you're doing barging in here like this?' His dark presence was overpowering in the tiny hallway, that raw, male magnetism a threat that made her pulses leap even while it sent warning signals to her brain. 'Didn't it ever occur to you to knock?'

The sapphire gaze flitted over her where she stood gripping the small Regency table behind her, and that uncompromising mouth pulled grimly. 'As a matter of fact, I did consider it,' he stated with hard emphasis, 'but in the circumstances I decided I probably wouldn't even get past the safety-chain.'

'You're darn right you wouldn't have!' It was a cry from the heart, strung with all the wounded pride she had suffered through her painful, adolescent love for him, and she gave a small gasp as tenacious fingers caught her wrist, pulling her to face him as she would have moved away.

'Why, Erica?' The subtle Scots tones grazed like sandpiper across her senses. 'Still not grown up enough yet to have shaken off those bourgeois prejudices? Or are you going to be daddy's little rich bitch until he partners you off with some brainless and pretentious little upstart who you imagine will be good enough to fit the bill?'

Angrily, she pulled away from him, ignoring his insults, colour suffusing her cheeks. He had called her a child before, when she had walked in on the scene of his infidelity, the sight of him, face flushed with passion as he clutched the stunning redhead on the settee, still cutting through her mind like a knife's serrated edge.

'Just how grown up does one have to be to accept that the man who's asked you to marry him has been seducing your father's wife as well?' It was all there in that one statement, the bitter pain she had nursed over the years. She had run upstairs—she remembered, fleetingly—hurting too much to stay and face them both, though Rafe had come after her, his voice deepening with anger when she'd refused to listen to what he had been trying to say.

Still, she'd thought him beneath her, anyway—cruelly, he'd thrown that at her then—which was obviously why she hadn't accepted his proposal. So what more could she expect from a man who wasn't even good enough to marry her?

She'd felt as if her heart had been torn out of her, her wounds taking a long time to heal, even in the quiet serenity of Switzerland. Then Laverne had had that accident—a simple yet fatal fall resulting in a broken neck—only four years after her marriage to Sir Joshua Witney, and Erica had never told him of Rafe's indiscriminate advances towards his wife.

She saw his eyes darken, then, incredibly, that cynical smile curl his lips. 'Yes ... well ... it gave you the excuse you needed to get away from me, didn't it?' he answered, with a scathing softness.

Was that what he had thought? Something of the agony she had known then surfaced with the poignant reminder that she had never let him know how much she had loved him—that she had kept her true feelings hidden with the secret of her inadequacy. And she was glad now that she had.

'You were right about something, Rafe—I *was* naïve,' she admitted, drawing herself up to her full height, though he still towered a good head over her. 'Still ...' a slim shoulder lifted, and bitterly ' ... we all change in five years, don't we?'

'Like your taste in men?'

His cool, derisory comment had Erica catching her breath, her lips thinning as she looked up into the cruel, hard beauty of his features. His remark was too personal, threatening to carry her over ground she had no wish to retrace. 'What's that supposed to mean?' Blast! Why did her voice have to shake?

The sagacity of his smile caused an uncomfortable heat to steal across her skin, feeling, as she did, that astute male perception tuned to her every weakness. 'Rather affectionate with that Caddis chap in the car park, weren't we?' he stated, a muscle working spasmodically in the strong jaw. And when she looked at him questioningly, he enlarged rather impatiently, 'I went to your office first, since I didn't know where you lived, and just happened to see you going to your car. It was only a question then of following you home.'

'How convenient for you!' she snapped, moving away from the table, considering that he must have done so with amazing discretion because she hadn't been aware of anyone following her.

'Well?' he queried softly, making her turn with a light movement of blonde hair, her fine brows knitting. 'Do I take it things are as serious between you and that boy-friend as they obviously appear?'

Beneath the thick sable of his lashes his eyes were probing—much too compelling—and she swallowed, feeling their impenetrable regard stripping her raw.

'So?' she responded quickly, suddenly desperate that he should believe it, gripping her small clutch-bag so tightly that her fingers ached.

'And you really think you can be happy with your father's lap-dog?' he queried with hard derogation. 'The sort who's only out for himself—furthering his own advancement by grovelling to the right people? I would have thought you could have done better for yourself, Erica, than an obvious yes-man like that?'

'How dare you say that about Graham?' Her brown eyes glittered hotly as she leaped to her friend's defence. 'You don't know anything about him. He's hard-working and honest, and, above all, he's loyal to the people he cares about!' she threw at him with a small catch in her voice, and pivoted away, only to be brought up short when he reached the lounge door before she did, his arm across the aperture, barring her way.

The near collision with that potent masculinity was more unsettling than she wanted to admit, and she saw him smile lazily, wise to her unease.

'And does he make you purr with desire, my dearest? Drive you mad for him the way I did? After all, you were never the type to settle for anything...below expectations...were you?'

She was about to rebel against the contempt in his words—in his eyes—but a cool hand against her cheek had her drawing in her breath. Numbly, she heard the hum of the fridge as it came on in the kitchen, her body sapping of energy as those long fingers trailed lightly down her throat. Something electric leaped through her at his touch, her heart pounding like a deafening sea in her ears. But with her pulses racing, she used all her strength to push at him hard with a biting, tremulous, 'Get lost!' brushing past him into the lounge.

'Oh no. Not this time, Erica.'

The steel behind the velvet of his voice made her skin prickle as she switched on the light, but she told herself not to be silly. What could he do?

Tossing her coat and bag down, caustically she threw over her shoulder, 'Why the hell did you come here, anyway?'

He didn't answer, looking around as if the simple though tastefully furnished flat surprised him, so different was it from the elaborate Surrey mansion she'd shared with her father before. But on her return from Switzerland she'd felt the need for independence—to break away from the trappings of luxury that had helped label her 'the Witney heiress' which she hated—and this small ground-floor flat suited her perfectly. Now she could feel that gaze running over the white sweater and dark, slimline skirt she wore, that leisurely male appraisal totally discomfiting.

'Sit down.'

His tone commanded, for all its softness, and, resenting that authority in him, Erica remained standing, her chin held defiantly in the air. He noted that little act of rebellion with the barest movement of an eyebrow, but said nothing, dropping down into an easy chair.

'Well?' she queried frostily.

He settled back against the floral cloth, chin resting on steepled hands, viewing her with a slow appreciation that even while it brought hot colour to her cheeks assured her he had no intention of being hurried. He looked tougher, she considered in that moment—much more ruthless than the teasing, tutoring lover she had known before—the lines of maturity etching his eyes and mouth somehow only adding to his attraction. The strong structure of forehead, cheek and jaw was sculpted with a forcefulness of character that had made him king in a cut-throat jungle, drawing the opposite sex to him with all the sway that five years ago had ensnared both her and her unfortunate stepmother, only now there seemed to be something almost lethal behind that dark sexuality.

Those eyes, catching the nervous movement of her throat, flickered with awareness. 'You know, you were right at court today, Erica,' he said then. 'I *can* help your father.'

She looked at him quickly, frowning. 'How? I thought you said you couldn't. That your father never talked——'

'He didn't,' was his hard reiteration. 'He was, however, very meticulous about keeping his own personal record of any significant developments he made in the lab. I can lay my hands on enough documentation that will get your father off the hook with no trouble at all—show that his claims are justified and that formula MG3 was discovered at *his* company. However...' He eased further back into his chair with an infuriating indolence as if he belonged there, clutching the long leg he brought up across his knee.

'However what?' Erica prompted a little uneasily, aware that his action had exposed the suggestion of a very masculine leg above the dark sock.

His gaze raked over her face, hard and assessing. 'There *is* a price.'

She might have known it! After all, she already knew him to be an opportunist. Outside, she heard the purr of a car engine as it turned into the square, then died on the other side of the park.

'What sort of price?' she demanded, a sick feeling curling in her stomach. He hardly needed money, surely? So what...?

His eyes rested on hers, glittering coldly, his contempt for her manifesting itself in its stark nakedness now. 'You think your money and social position holds the answer to everything, don't you?' he said thickly, as if reading her thoughts. 'But quite honestly, Erica, I'm not impressed by them—I never was. What I want from you, dearest, can't be measured in sterling...exactly...' He got up then, his hard, athletic grace with that unmistakable verbal threat sending a little trickle of fear through her, so that she brought her tongue nervously across her top lip.

'What do you mean?' she queried cagily, her hands moving into tight little fists.

He came towards her, hands on his hips, the dark, gaping jacket exposing the pristine whiteness of his shirt, the hard, lean angles of his body. 'I'll provide that information, but in return I want a chunk of Witneys—and I'll expect a good chunk,' he stated decisively, his mouth firming in hard, uncompromising lines.

'Oh, will you?' she spat on a tight, brittle little laugh, his sheer audacity making her hackles rise. 'And don't you think my father will have something to say about that?'

'Your father's already expressed an interest in my active involvement with the company,' dismayed she heard him saying. 'Let's not fool ourselves,' he advised grimly. 'Witneys isn't doing as well as it should at present, and it seems to me Sir Joshua would welcome a man who can be trusted to look after his company's interests—and his daughter's,' he interjected drily. 'Especially someone who can lend an experienced hand to a badly needed restructuring of the firm with guaranteed results.'

'Oh, I'm sure he would—and with open arms!' she retorted with scornful acidity. 'Especially if he knew how you played around with his wife!' Her breasts rose sharply from the deep well of bitterness inside her, the fine features tense from the effort of concealing just how deeply he had hurt her before.

That grim, male countenance took on an almost savage expression, and he seemed to stiffen with some ugly emotion she could almost feel.

'But you're hardly likely to tell him, are you, Erica?' The low warning in his voice was intimidating as he took a step towards her, the sapphire eyes glittering with a hard challenge. 'You might take first prize for your total disregard for anyone who isn't on the same social ladder as you are, but I would have hoped telling a man of his dead wife's infidelity would be stretching things a bit— even for you.' The soft hatred in his voice flayed across her raw nerves, and she tried to speak, but he didn't give her the chance, a cold implacability making his eyes glint like hard steel as he went on, 'Naturally, your father isn't too keen on giving a controlling share to anyone outside the family circle, but, similarly, I don't want to dedicate precious time to something where I'm not going to see a valuable return at the end of the day. He could probably get the company back on course, I'm sure, without my help—through any number of consultants— but not if he's got too many other worries—such as whether or not he's going to be labelled a thief at the end of the day. Therefore, it rests with you, my beautiful, heartless little cat; it rests on whether you want to see your father's health and reputation totally destroyed or not. But if you want me to help him...provide the court with that evidence...' His hesitation was deliberate, his smile cruelly relishing. 'You're going to have to marry me first!'

CHAPTER TWO

'YOU can't be serious!' Erica exhaled, flopping down into a chair, heart pounding, her throat going dry. 'I'd rather die first!' she threw at Rafe bitingly, turning away.

Some emotion darkened his eyes, lent a tautness to the proud austerity of his proile. 'Perhaps ... but it isn't your life that's at stake here, is it?' he reminded her stoically, so much in control that she shivered from the cold-blooded calculation behind his words. 'I understand your father's health isn't too good these days. That his doctors have said another heart attack could be fatal. It isn't going to help matters much if he has to spend any length of time in prison.'

Flinching, she shot a frightened glance his way. She had never really let herself believe that it could come to that, but now the possibility of it filled her with cold, sickening dread. 'You wouldn't let that happen,' she whispered up at him, apprehension coiling with inexplicable pain inside her from the suspicion that he might just be capable of it.

'Don't credit me with qualities that I don't possess, sweetheart—I'm no sentimentalist,' he assured her coolly. 'But I would have thought you'd have wanted to help your father in any way you could.'

Yes, but not by marrying a man she despised!

'Rafe, be reasonable...' There was supplication in her eyes, her nails unconsciously curling into the soft fabric arms of her chair. 'I'll do anything to help Dad, but you can't expect me to agree to something like what you're suggesting. I'll pay you for that information. I'll pay you anything!' she entreated desperately. 'Only don't ask me to——'

'No, Erica.' The Scots tones were soft but inexorable. 'I've stated my terms. It's marriage or nothing.' He shrugged, the casual gesture belying the determination in him—the hard, mercenary power. 'It's your choice.'

She looked at him from under her lashes, at the implacable lines of his strong, dark face, that commanding maleness of him making her shudder.

'Some choice!' she snapped, loathing him—wondering how he could possibly treat her like this. Had it been such a blow to his ego five years ago when he'd believed she'd thought him beneath her that male pride was now forcing him to prove that she could still be his for the taking? Or, she wondered, with a heart-spearing anguish taking her breath away, did he really see her merely as a means to a satisfactory financial end?

She closed her eyes against the emotion that stung them, blotting out his lean, dark-suited figure. 'What is it you want, Rafe?' she enquired softly when she could face him again. 'Revenge?' Then recklessly, 'Did it goad that much having to come to terms with exactly what you are?'

A powerful shoulder lifted. 'And what's that?' he returned grazingly. 'The adulterer you like to think I am? Or the plebeian who wasn't fit to share anything with you beyond those basic physical pleasures of yours?'

His words flayed, colour staining her cheeks. But, of course, he didn't know the real reason for her not accepting his proposal, she thought, anguished—why she couldn't bring herself to trap him in a marriage which would have denied him the children he'd wanted—because she'd loved him so much.

For one rash, hurting moment she almost told him to stick his help—that she didn't need it. But she did. He held the only key that could unlock the truth to clear

Sir Joshua, but what he was asking in return was totally preposterous.

'I'm offering you the chance of saving your father's reputation...perhaps even his life,' he reminded her quietly when she remained silent, and he came over to her then, stooping to place his hands on either side of her chair, his sudden, unexpected nearness making her heart thud. She caught the elusive scent of his cologne, eyes drawn to the hard texture of his skin, the strong jaw, the cruel sensuality of his mouth, recognising, with a shaming intensity, that familiar, traitorous ache for him deep in her loins. 'Isn't that what you want?' She couldn't meet his eyes, trapped in some lethal prison of the senses, and when she didn't answer he said, 'If you agree, we'll be married as soon as possible. We'll have a honeymoon first for us to...' his mouth firmed, sending small, unwelcome tingles along her spine '...break the ice, and afterwards, when I decide, I'll provide my evidence.' Suddenly he stood up, releasing her from the time-locked spell of that dangerous magnetism. 'If you don't...'

If she didn't, then her father could go hang! That was what he was saying, she realised, her senses returning with a pointless anger now that he had put more space between them again. Even so, tossing her hair back from her face, her chin in the air, astringently she challenged, 'And if I don't, and I tell Dad's solicitor you're holding evidence that could get Dad off the hook, you'll deny it—naturally?'

A thick eyebrow lifted, although he didn't say a word. He didn't need to, she thought, through a cold, sickening despair.

She didn't know how she got through the next few days. Even the challenge of her job had lost its immediate appeal, and now, sitting behind her desk in her small, modern office, Erica stared at the open file in front of her without digesting a word.

Rafe had told her to think over his proposal and she had—to the exclusion of practically everything else! Her father needed help—a help only Rafe could give him. But what he was demanding in return was unimaginable—totally out of the quesion! How could she marry him? she asked herself bleakly, memory, like some sophisticated Chinese torture, piercing through her as she relived his brutal betrayal with Laverne.

Elbows on the desk, she pressed her palms against the wells of her eyes, trying with a hopeless futility not to think about it—to blot out other memories of that summer. He had been so tender with her in those days— reluctantly she recalled—at other times, so mind- blowingly passionate, while she, naïve and adoring, had imagined his feelings for her were as strong as hers had been for him, because like her he had never actually de- clared them openly. But had he really loved her before he'd arrived at those unjustified conclusions about her? Before she'd driven him unwittingly into the willing arms of her stepmother?

A small sob caught in her throat as she realised that she'd been through this torturous, soul-searching in- trospection before, wondering if she hadn't been partly— even wholly—to blame. But if he had loved her, how could he use her love for her father now as a means of trying to get her to agree to his demands, she asked herself bitterly—just for his own financial gain? And if she didn't . . .

She shivered, not wanting to think about the conse- quences—of how ill Sir Joshua had looked before he'd left for Yorkshire—her worries only intensifying when she stepped into his office that afternoon and saw him sitting at his desk, glass in hand, taking one of his tablets, looking flushed and tired, despite his few days away.

'Not feeling well, Dad?' she enquired, a sympathetic smile hiding the true extent of her concern.

He seemed to perk up a little when he saw her crossing the plush office—an office Rafe had designs on, she couldn't help reminding herself bitterly.

'Oh, it's only the usual, love. I'm getting too old and weary for this job, I'm afraid. It needs a younger man with more drive and enthusiasm to give the company the sort of boost it needs if we're to restore some of the confidence we've lost over this infernal MG3 thing both at home and abroad.'

'Like Rafe Cameron?' she queried pointedly, her pulse-rate suddenly increasing.

'Have you seen him?' he asked, with a sidelong, almost hopeful look at his daughter.

'Yes,' she breathed, colour touching her cheeks. 'Why didn't you tell me you'd been talking to him?' she quizzed, her expression hurt, unable to believe he had actually been discussing Witneys' future—hers—with Rafe. 'You don't usually keep company affairs from me like that.'

'I wasn't sure how you'd take it, love. You were pretty heavily involved with him before.'

'Is that why you gave him the impression I needed looking after?' she enquired, rather more sharply than she intended.

He made a careless gesture with his hand, blue eyes concerned beneath his white hair. 'I probably mentioned it in passing,' was all he was admitting. 'Why?'

Erica's breast lifted under her creamy blouse. 'Because he's asked me to marry him,' she exhaled with a tremor she couldn't conceal.

'Has he, love?' Her father's face seemed to shine like the silver trophies in the cabinet behind his chair—prizes from the amateur golf tournaments he had won in his youth—making him look younger, less strained. 'I hope you're not going to be foolish enough to let him get away again.' He smiled, unaware of the way she flinched. He didn't know that it had been she who had ended the relationship last time, or even that Rafe had proposed to her before. Foolishly, she had shared that little confidence only with her stepmother, desperate as she'd been for another woman's advice all those years ago...

'You could do far worse,' Sir Joshua was advising soberly, mistaking the tautening of her features from a sudden, very private anguish for instant rebellion on her part. 'His father was a brilliant man, and Rafe's inherited that brilliance—tenfold if his business record is anything to go by. Besides, there isn't a man I'd trust more with my company—or my daughter,' he stated with an emphasis that made Erica bristle simply from imagining herself under Rafe Cameron's controlling influence. 'And at least with Rafe you know he wouldn't be marrying you just because of your money.'

No, but he wanted power over her—her humiliation—and in marrying her he would have that, she realised, pique flaring as she thought about it. And a few more millions to add to those he already had wasn't exactly going to hurt him any!

Oh, Dad! If only you knew! She turned away, unable to look at him—a prisoner of her own painful secrets, because she couldn't ever tell him about Laverne, about Rafe's little regard for him, about the evidence he was threatening to withhold if she didn't marry him.

'If you did tie the knot with Rafe,' Sir Joshua continued to press as Erica handed him a file, 'I know it's a pretty long shot, but if the two of you were ever to produce a baby, think what a little scientific genius it could well turn out to be!'

'Oh, *Dad*!' He didn't intend to be tactless. He was simply being carried away by his own hopes for the future, she reasoned unhappily, but it hurt—like hell.

His keenness, though, for her to marry Rafe, only served to put added pressure on her, intensifying the conflict inside her. To disappoint her father by not marrying the man he wanted her to marry was one thing, she reflected, as she made her way back to her own offfice. But to stand by and see him being persecuted because of this formula dispute, possibly even winding up in prison when she had the power to prevent it . . .

She shuddered, hating Rafe Cameron in that moment more than she'd imagined it was possible to hate anyone, angry tears burning her eyes as she acknowledged that, really, she had very little choice. She'd have to comply with him if she wanted to help her father, she thought acidly, anger and fear and despair closing in on her with that final acceptance of defeat.

Stepping out of the shower, and slipping into a short, red silk wrap, Erica started, hearing the peal of the doorbell.

Graham! she realised queasily. She'd asked him to come round tonight so that she could break it to him very gently about Rafe because she knew he would be upset. And now he'd arrived early!

As she opened the door, though, a gasp escaped her, her appearance bringing a wry twist to her visitor's lips.

'Well, well. Do you often make a point of answering the door looking like this, or is this solely for my benefit?'

Rafe's sardonic drawl made her hackles rise, as did the way he stepped in uninvited, although the sight of him in a light grey lounge suit, white shirt and silver tie took her breath away. That, and the fact that she was almost naked under the little flimsy wrap she was wearing!

'You would be conceited enough to think that, wouldn't you?' she spat, swinging away from him on legs that suddenly felt like jelly.

He followed her in, his gaze drawn to the vivid pink of some lovingly tended cyclamen plants on the lounge window-sill, before coming to rest on Erica again. 'Not conceit, my love... merely a process of elimination. Sir Joshua came back from Yorkshire today, which would have given you the opportunity of discussing your decision with him if you've been sensible enough to make the right one. Therefore I would have thought it obvious to you that naturally I'd be calling round tonight.'

She hated him—his self-assurance, the way he held his head at that arrogant tilt—and with a swift movement that brought her damp hair tumbling out of its top-knot in a golden cloud she said bitterly, 'Why? So you can move in for the kill?'

Anger darkened his eyes to a cold, inky blue. Then it vanished, replaced by an incandescent glitter that made her pulse throb, her throat go dry. 'That isn't how I would describe making love to you.'

Inevitably, she blushed, and against her will felt that age-old ache of desire for him swell in the pit of her stomach. His gaze fell, mouth twitching in awareness, and she knew that the urgent swell of her breasts against the soft silk had betrayed her to him. She made to move away, only to realise it was a mistake when she found herself trapped by the lightning reflexes of his hand.

She was pulled up against him, and gave a small gasp of shock as he bent his dark head to the little throbbing hollow of her throat, her body seeming to liquefy as his lips burned a heart-stopping trail across the open V of her wrap.

For one breathless moment she wanted to arch against him, her fingers clutching tensely at his sleeves. His mouth, his scent, the familiar, solid warmth of him filled

her with treacherous longing, but one small shred of
sanity remained so that she pulled back, her memories
too bitter—too strong.

'Let me go!'

'No.' His hands tightened around her upper arms, the
strong features unyielding and hard. 'You want me—
you still want me—no matter how much that stubborn
little brain of yours tries to veto it.' There was a deep
flush across the taut olive skin, and those blue eyes were
so darkly probing that she lowered hers, staring at the
shadow of crisp, dark hair beneath the fine silk of his
shirt. 'Something sparked between us the instant we met
again in that court last week, and, try though you might
to make me believe otherwise, you felt it too. I'm not
blind to a thing like that.'

'Well, no, you've had a lot of practice, haven't you?'
she retorted acridly. 'And not always with people who
were free for the taking, either!'

Anger blanching his skin, his fingers dug into her soft
flesh, and for an instant she thought he was going to
shake her for making that last, impetuous remark. But
then he released her and, with surprising calmness, said
simply, 'Well?'

He was asking for her decision, she realised, features
rebellious, meeting the impenetrable strength of his with
a dryness scorching her throat. 'If you mean do you get
a wife solely through emotional blackmail and who'll
despise you for it for life, then I suppose the answer's
yes!' she flung at him bitterly, although she had to lower
her lashes against the betraying turmoil in her eyes,
breathing in a scathing whisper, 'You're loathsome!'

'Yes,' he exhaled in agreement, forcing her head up
by catching her small chin between his thumb and forefinger with a cruel pressure that made her wince. 'And
don't look so childishly hurt. As I said before, you can
hardly expect any less from a man who wasn't good

enough for you—to father your children—can you?' His tongue flayed her raw, the hatred in those implacable features firing an answering antagonism in her so that her lips tightened mutinously, every nerve rebelling against a sick excitement from the burning touch of his hand. 'Well you'll have my children, Erica—and like it— that will be part of the deal. And I'll expect you to provide me with our first as soon as possible after the wedding.'

'Oh, really!' Colour stained her cheeks and temples as she sent a mutinous look up at him, about to blurt out that that was what he thought, that in all probability she'd never be able to have any children, but she stopped herself in time. He was so darned arrogant, let him find it out for himself! He might be giving her no other option to help her father, but at least, now, she realised, she had a very effective weapon with which she could pay him back. She'd agree to all his terms. The marriage. The honeymoon. And any other darn stipulation he cared to make! Then the day he cleared her father's name, she would drop her bombshell. And what a rude awakening he'd have—finding out he'd lumbered himself with a sterile wife!

'You'll do as I say,' he promised smoothly, the relentless determination in him making her shiver, wondering as she was how he might deal with her when he eventually discovered the truth. 'Quite frankly, I don't give a darn whether you like it or not, but at least your father will be pleased.'

'Well, yes, but he doesn't know you as I do, does he, Rafe?' she taunted, lifting her head proudly in a silver cloud of defiance to hide a sudden bout of nerves. And paid for it when his hand slid down to the outer curve of her breast, cupping the soft mound.

'No,' he countered silkily, those dark features smug from the involuntary response her body conveyed to him—from the short, sharp catching of her breath. 'You don't know me at all, my sweet. But you're going to, I promise. Very intimately and very well. By the time I've finished with you, Erica, you aren't going to care whether I was dragged up in the gutter or beamed in from another planet. I'll have respect from you if it's only through that one area of weakness that even you, my love, can't do anything about. Desire.'

Little goose-bumps broke out across her flesh, and she bit her lip against the stimulating warmth of his hand. He was too dangerous a man to play around with, she advised herself with trembling caution, and she was still too vulnerable to that raw, masculine sexuality, wondering with a gnawing anxiety if she was wise in going ahead with such a reckless plan to pay him back. Just how he might react was something she didn't want to think about or she'd never be able to go through with it, she realised, so tense that she almost leapt with fright when the doorbell rang again.

Graham! With heart-sinking dismay she realised she had forgotten he was coming, and wondered how on earth she was going to explain things now that Rafe was there.

Pivoting away from him, she went to answer the door, hoping against hope that she could persuade Graham to come back a little later when she was dressed. That way she could then ask Rafe to leave so that she could tell Graham about him in less embarrassing circumstances. Rafe owed her that much privacy at least. But when she opened the door, Graham was too eager, stepping inside and immediately pulling her into his arms with an unusual and unwelcome ardour he made no attempt to conceal.

'Gosh, Erica...do you know what you do to me looking like this?'

She did, and she was trying desperately to put a stop to it, but not half as effectively as the deep, masculine voice that drifted down the hallway towards them.

'I'm sorry, Caddis, but you seem to be infringing upon my territorial rights.'

How dared he? And referring to her as if she were some property he owned! He was coming towards them with the self-assured stride of a man who had every right to be there, and the abhorrent look Erica shot him changed to a silent, desperate apology as she turned back to Graham.

'What's going on?'

He didn't need to be told. He had arrived at his own conclusions, she realised hopelessly, seeing his impassioned features whiten as he looked from her scantily clad figure to the imposing elegance of the man beside her. It hadn't been her intention to hurt him, but she had, she thought despairingly, flinching as Rafe slipped a proprietorial arm around her waist.

'Hasn't she told you?' He pulled her hard and possessively against him, rendering further explanation unnecessary. She became startlingly alive to the hard bone and muscle of his hip and thigh, to the warmth of his hand burning against her abdomen through the thin silk, and in a half-daze she heard him clarifying, 'We're going to be married.' There was cool victory in his eyes as he looked down at her, adding with a click of his tongue, 'How remiss of you not to let him know, darling.'

She could have hit him, her chaotic thoughts preventing her from saying anything as Graham gave her one chillingly searching look and stormed back to his car.

She was unable to believe that she could let Rafe do this to her—take such complete control of her life—and as the car screeched away something seemed to explode inside her and her hands came up in tight little fists to pummel him hard on the chest.

'You bastard! You unfeeling bastard!' Angry tears were collecting in her eyes as she struck out at him, hurting herself more than she was hurting him as she met a wall of relentless muscle that refused to yield.

'No, Erica, my parents *were* married,' he reminded her, half amused, unperturbed by her ungainly protests, 'even if they did split up shortly after I came on the scene.'

Suddenly, though, he decided he'd taken enough, dragging her hands down and holding them behind her back while she lamented bitterly, eyes blazing beneath her wet lashes, 'Did you *have* to interfere? Send him away like that?' He'd been a dear friend, after all.

'Yes.' He took a deep breath, one hand tangling in the thick cascade of blonde hair, pulling her head back so that her small, insurgent features were openly exposed to his. 'I'm a jealous lover, Erica. I object to finding my fiancée in another man's arms. I was simply ensuring that it didn't happen again.'

She wanted to retaliate, but couldn't, shocked, as his arms locked her to him, to realise that even in anger she had aroused him. Her breath caught in her lungs, heart thudding as he claimed her mouth with his, the familiar intimacy of his scent, his warmth, the hard possession of his embrace sparking that fundamental need of him to vibrant life inside her, even as she tensed rigid, determined to resist. His kiss, though, was long and leisurely, that burning male mouth exploring the moist cavern of hers with an insidious expertise that left her breathless—hands freed yet helpless against his chest as she fought to hang on to her control, although she was visibly trembling when he released her.

'I detest you,' she got out shakily, her face flushed, her breasts rising and falling sharply beneath the red wrap.

'Perhaps,' he conceded, the twist of triumph on his lips proof that he was in no doubt as to the effort of will it had taken for her not to capitulate to his kiss. 'But whether you're in love with Caddis or not, there's something between us, Erica, that even you can't deny...something that's always been there. I would have thought, in the circumstances, you would have regarded that as an advantage. They say physical compatibility isn't everything in a relationship, but it certainly goes towards making up a very important part.'

So he thought she was in love with the other man. Well, let him think it! she decided acridly, retorting unthinkingly with a careless, 'I wouldn't know.'

A dark eyebrow lifted as he scanned the small, proud features, a thin line creasing his forehead. 'Are you trying to tell me you're still as innocent as that pleading little seventeen-year-old I couldn't be heel enough to give into?' Incredulity lit the blue eyes, but his flippant, shaming reminder of how willingly she had offered herself to him—of how much she had loved him—cut her to the quick, and with a flood of embarrassed colour in her cheeks she was flinging back, 'That's none of your damn business!'

'Don't be ridiculous,' he drawled.

Which she was being, she admitted tremblingly to herself. After all, very soon he would know for himself.

'Then you'll just have to wait and find out, won't you?' she parried, but suddenly she felt all in—tired from this continual, fruitless contention with him—and wearily she leaned back against the wall.

Under the soft light from one of the wall lamps, a shadow flitted across the strongly chiselled face. 'Don't you think I've already waited for you long enough?' His words barely above a whisper, he was reaching for her, sending fear and excitement leaping through her as she recognised the naked hunger in his eyes. But then he was saying with a sudden, husky quality to his voice, 'One thing I do have in common with your dear Graham is that your looking like this isn't doing me any good, either. Go and get dressed,' he advised, and, with noticeable reluctance, released her. 'I'm taking you out to dinner.'

She obeyed instantly, glad to get away from him, wondering how on earth she would ever be able to endure such an intimacy with him as marriage would demand without revealing just how susceptible she still was to him. The flesh had no morals like the mind, otherwise how could she still be so strongly affected by him? A man who had seduced her own stepmother, she reminded herself poignantly, despising herself for her weakness, her conscience only appeased by the thought of his futile anger when he discovered the truth about her.

The next couple of weeks sped by too quickly, and they were the most miserable of Erica's life. It was difficult trying to look happy when everyone admired the cluster of diamonds that shone so brilliantly on her finger, when making numb responses to the flood of reporters who invaded her home and her office, jostling for the most sensational story of how the Witney heiress had hooked one of Britain's most eligible millionaires. Graham avoided her entirely. As for Rafe, he was engaged in the final stages of some job abroad, returning at the beginning of the second week to spin her into a whirlwind courtship, while putting the final seal on the plans Erica had had no desire to make.

'You two couldn't have made me happier,' Sir Joshua enthused, leaving Erica's flat one afternoon just as Rafe was arriving to keep their appointment with the photographer.

He slapped the younger man's shoulder in confirmation on his way down to the waiting Rolls, and Erica ignored the cool victory in the sapphire eyes, pulling on gloves that matched a pure woollen navy-blue suit before saying crisply, 'Well? Shall we go?'

He seemed unaffected by her unfriendly tone, his manners impeccable as he opened the door of the white BMW for her, the perfect ease of his stride as he came around the bonnet, like his appearance, totally devastating.

A week's tropical sun had deepened the olive of the easily tanned skin, complementing the black hair and brows and the light tan of the anorak he wore over snug-fitting trousers which emphasised the firmness of long, well-muscled legs. Every bit the man in command—in control—Erica thought, resenting him as much as the way her stomach muscles contracted so that she was quick to glance away as he climbed in beside her, savouring, with a bitter-sweet taste in her mouth, the prospect of her revenge when she told him the chances of his having any children with her were as good as nil.

It was an agreeable afternoon—or would have been if this had been an engagement she'd been enjoying— because the sun shone for a while, making the outward journey pleasant, and the photographer, after settling the wedding arrangements, and obviously imagining them to be deeply in love, insisted they join him in a glass of sherry.

'Well that's that,' Rafe announced when they were motoring back. 'Everything's arranged.' And with a crooked smile in her direction, 'Unless you can think of anything we've overlooked.'

'Well, if we have, you'll just have to discover it for yourself!' she snapped unhelpfully, refusing to cooperate with him over the details of a wedding she didn't want. 'And yes, there is something,' she decided tartly after a few moments, watching the movement of his long hand as he flicked the switch for the sidelights because dusk was falling now. 'How do I even know that you've got that evidence you claim to have that can help Dad? Don't you think it's about time I had some proof that it even exists?'

'No,' he said succinctly then, bringing the powerful car back into the square where she lived. 'I'm afraid you're just going to have to take my word for it. After all, they do say the best marriages are those that are based on trust.'

She swallowed, suddenly feeling surprisingly guilty. Despite the cynical way he'd said that, she knew he meant it, just as she knew, instinctively, that whatever else he did he would never lie. But as he pulled up outside her flat, conscience had her flinging back rather heatedly, 'Maybe. But it's hardly going to be a normal marriage, is it?'

'I'm afraid you're wrong, Erica.' His words held a daunting resolve as he applied the handbrake, turning to bring his arm across the back of her seat with a tantalising waft of his cologne. 'I intend to see that it's entirely normal—from the little ecstasies we're going to share to the children we're going to have—so you'd better get used to the idea.'

'Oh, had I?' Her hair gleamed like pale silk in the now almost dark interior of the car as she faced him in unarmed combat, anger forcing her to respond, 'Aren't you presuming a lot? You might be able to order *me* around, but you can't order Nature around! Some women can't——' She stopped dead, suddenly in danger of saying too much, and she felt an uncomfortable, clammy heat steal over her as those dark brows came together, as Rafe studied her with hard, unnerving scrutiny.

'If you've got any doubts on that score, Erica, perhaps we'd better get a few tests done,' horrified she heard him suggest, the fear that he might now insist upon it contending with the stabbing realisation that he could be so cold-blooded. Tears stung her eyes, and she was stumbling out of the car, ashamed to let him see—to even admit to herself—that he still had the power to hurt her.

'What's wrong?' he prompted when he had joined her on the top step, taking the key from her fingers that were trembling too much to unlock the door, opening it himself.

She made to go inside, but he stalled her, the hand that turned her face to his surprisingly gentle, although he seemed to catch his breath, the planes of that strong face tautening with some dark emotion when he noticed the tiny beads glistening on her lower lids.

'Saturday's going to come, dearest, whether you want it to or not,' he breathed almost hoarsely, clearly misunderstanding the reason for her melancholy. 'You're going to be my wife as I intended five years ago—but don't worry. You can rest assured I'm not going to beat you.' Which was supposed to be comforting! she supposed, her colour rising, but before she could find some apt retort his lips were against her brow. 'You're overwrought. Get an early night,' he recommended, almost solicitously, his breath against her skin sending a dart of antagonised excitement through her so that she shuddered as she watched him stride away.

However would she remain immune to that dark sexuality when the merest touch from him made her tremble? she wondered, sick at herself, dreading this forthcoming marriage. And now the revenge she'd been planning looked like backfiring on her, she berated herself, simply because she hadn't been able to control her angry tongue. But would he insist on those tests? Talons of anxiety tightened around her stomach as she considered what would happen if he did. He certainly wouldn't consider marrying her when he found out the truth, which would mean he'd probably refuse to help her father, too, she realised, stifling a small sob from the agonising knowledge that he could be so mercenary, praying, as she turned into the flat, that she could keep her secret from him at least until he'd cleared Sir Joshua's name.

It was a tall, pale figure she presented that Saturday morning to her father, who was waiting patiently for her in the large hall of his magnificent house.

He looked splendid in his grey morning suit, she thought, somehow managing to smile, determined to keep her true emotions hidden from him and her excited, bubbly bridesmaids—two friends from the office dressed in striking peacock-blue.

She had wanted a quiet wedding at the local register office with few guests—a simple, meaningless exchange of words befitting the farce of the marriage she was entering into. But Rafe had insisted on the full paraphernalia—church, a long list of guests, formal dress. And so she had gone over the top almost in spite of herself in the short time she had had, choosing the flounciest, most expensive gown she could find, looking like a modern day Cinderella beneath the tumbling layers of silk—a happy Cinderella about to be joined with her Prince Charming—so that only she knew the reason for her bloodless complexion beneath the elegantly coiled honey of her hair.

'You look beautiful, my darling.' Her father's lips on her cheek brought a painful lump to her throat, and to hide her emotion she busied herself with straightening a recalcitrant veil, knowing that if she'd said anything at that moment she might just have broken down—re-

vealed how unhappy she was—and she had to go through
with this marriage for *his* sake.

'Going down with guns blazing?' was Rafe's amused
whisper when she joined him at the altar, and she looked
away from those too perceptive eyes, down at her
bouquet, the florist's words as she had ordered that
startling contrast of colours coming sharply to her mind.

'Bad luck,' the woman had stated drily. 'An ill omen.'
Which couldn't have been more appropriate for her,
Erica had thought. And staring down at the vivid red
roses against the stark white of the feathery carnations,
she could see why. They looked like fire against ice—
blood against virgin snow...

The service was a trauma which was over before she
had realised it, the photographs, reception and exchanges with well-wishers an ordeal she could have done
without. All she remembered afterwards was a sea of
faces, friends—no family, as Sir Joshua and her mother
had, like her, been only children, but there were a couple
of distant relatives of Rafe's and, blowing her nose,
ashamed of tears that made her pretend she was nursing
a cold, the grey-haired little figure of Myrtle
Washbourne.

'Now you take care of her, Mr Cameron!' The
Yorkshire woman was wagging a gnarled finger at the
man. She was a kind, reliable friend who seemed to Erica
to have been widowed forever and who looked after their
holiday cottage, putting up with her, Erica remembered
fondly—even though childless herself—with patience and
understanding during all those long, lonely school holidays she'd spent in the North Country as a youngster.
'She's been like a daughter to me and I wouldn't have
welcomed her being carried off by just anybody. I'm
surprised you didn't make an honest woman of her
before now,' she sniffed, obviously approving, 'instead
of letting her run off to Switzerland like she did, filling

her head with that degree and that marketing business that in my day only lads wanted to know anything about. You must be a very patient man.'

The glittering question in Rafe's eyes had Erica glancing away, breath catching in her lungs. She knew exactly what he was thinking. Hadn't she told him five years ago that she'd wanted a good time before she settled down—a tasteless excuse she'd used when she'd felt pressurised into giving him an answer to his proposal? And, of course, Myrtle didn't know how bitter their break-up had been, she reflected poignantly—or how torn apart she'd been when she had fled away to Europe—so she could hardly blame the woman for saying what she had.

'No, not particularly patient, Myrtle,' she heard Rafe admitting then, and, looking up, caught his gaze fully and unexpectedly this time, its cool intensity taking no warmth from his smile as he supplied, 'Let's just say I've been waiting for the right opportunity.'

Yes, with my father's innocence as ransom! she thought hotly, through a bitter, deepening resentment, wishing for all the world that there could have been some other way to have cleared her father without her having to resort to accepting Rafe's help—agree to his demands.

But there wasn't, and you did, an inner little voice reminded—making her stomach churn—as she sat beside him on the plane. He hadn't actually said any more about her taking those fertility tests he'd mentioned when she'd been careless enough almost to let her secret out that night in his car, but she was still afraid that he might insist upon it, and with a little shudder, palms sticky with nerves, she stole a sideways glance at him.

He was ordering drinks from a glamorous young hostess, and from the girl's smiling attentiveness he might have been the most important passenger on the flight.

And how skilfully that inherent male charm disguised the steel-hard ruthlessness of his character, she marvelled, feeling almost sorry for the blushing hostess, wondering uneasily how long she'd be able to keep her secret from that shrewd, discerning brain. He was too clever to fool for any length of time, and if he insisted on those tests before she could persuade him to hand over that evidence—found out the truth about her...

She swallowed, and, glancing away to the sea of cloud beyond the small window, told herself that she had got herself in it up to her neck.

'Well...alone at last.' She started as the strong male hand caught hers, realising that the hostess had moved away. 'From here on, Erica Cameron, we can get to know each other again.'

She flinched at the linking of his name with hers, unsettlingly aware of his warm palm against her own.

'And carry on where we left off?' Delicate features lifted to his, eyes dark with inner turmoil.

'No.' One saturnine glance embraced her slenderness beneath a flattering red suit and cream silk blouse, the way those beautiful eyes lingered causing her skin to heat. 'I was thinking more of a new beginning—a completely fresh start with just the two of us. The past is dead. It's over.'

'And *conveniently* forgotten?' She couldn't restrain the taunt, the brutal hurt she had suffered through his cruel liaison with her stepmother stirring like a ghost that refused to die.

She heard him catch his breath, felt the sudden withdrawal of his hand before he rasped with quietly controlled anger, 'Say it any louder and the whole darn plane will hear.' There was a tenseness about him that gave a waxy quality to the skin stretched over his cheekbones, but then he seemed to relax a little, his mouth curving faintly as he studied the soft, strained angles of her face. 'Look happy for me, dearest.' His voice was suddenly coolly derisive. 'I'd hate for us to destroy everyone's illusion of the enraptured bride and groom embarking on a blissful honeymoon.'

She glanced across to the the middle-aged couple sitting opposite, and the woman smiled warmly at her before returning to a magazine.

'You've got far too vivid an imagination, Rafe,' she murmured drily, features controlled, her gaze wandering of its own accord over the taut, prominent line of his jaw. 'No one's imagining anything of the sort.'

Above the drone of the engines, she heard his low chuckle. 'No?' Those blue eyes embraced her, amused now—reflective—and suddenly his hand was lifting to her hair. Erica held her breath, stiffening from the unexpected contact, and she looked puzzlingly at him as gently he drew something from the soft strands.

It was a small red paper heart—perfectly shaped and fragile—one stray piece of confetti from a handful with which someone had showered them as they'd left the house. Stupidly, she felt a swift upsurge of emotion that brought a painful lump to her throat, and half ashamed she turned away. She had always imagined her wedding day would be a happy occasion, the one day when she would give herself wholly to a man she loved. Not this pain, this burning resentment she was taking with her on her honeymoon, shackled to a man she despised.

From under her lashes, numbly, she watched Rafe crush the tiny fragment between his thumb and forefinger, as brutally as he had crushed her adolescent love for him, and intuitively she knew that, whatever she had suffered through loving him in the past, there would be far worse to endure in the days and months ahead.

CHAPTER THREE

THE small Greek island Rafe had chosen for their honeymoon was a far cry from the tropical winter paradise to which he had originally offered to take Erica, the little white house standing in its narrow street in the mild sunshine so different from the luxury hotel she'd been envisaging. But when he had asked her where she had wanted to spend the ten-day honeymoon, rather ungraciously she'd informed him that she didn't care—that, as the marriage and the honeymoon were totally meaningless to her, he could go wherever he liked. And so he had arranged everything without divulging their exact destination until they had stepped off the plane, and now, looking up at the terracotta-roofed building with its backdrop of quiet, green forestry, silently Erica had to compliment him on his choice. Perhaps he had guessed how she would have hated facing people if they had stayed in a large hotel; how it would have been a strain for her to smile—look the part of the happy bride, radiant from the ecstasies of newly wedded bliss—and she looked at the dark-suited man at her side with a little twinge of apprehension as she considered the evening ahead. Well, at least here there was no one to witness the tension in her, she thought, wondering if he'd taken that into account, too. No one, except Alecco Stavros.

The broad, elderly Greek, clad in loose white shirt and trousers, hugged Rafe like a long-lost son as soon as they stepped through the door, his strong, weather-lined face breaking into a smile as he said in very accented English, 'And this your new—how you say—little

woman?' He caught Erica's hand, shaking it whole-
heartedly—too polite to treat her with the same familiarity he had shown Rafe—and, with a glance over her
figure, was murmuring something obviously approving
in Greek, before adding with a knowing wink at Rafe,
'She will give you many babies.'

Erica stiffened, hoping that Rafe wouldn't notice the
guilty colour that crept into her cheeks as he responded
in a voice laced with amusement, 'I'm sure Mrs Cameron
would agree that one will be quite adequate to begin
with.'

Something leaped in those blue eyes—something
sensual and challenging, making her throat contract—
and abstractedly she heard Alecco laugh. 'That's what
I mean...one at a time,' he amended, murmuring
apologies for his English.

She saw Rafe's understanding smile and forced her
lips to imitate his, though she was relieved when Alecco
decided it was time to go, wishing them well and informing them that his wife had left fresh bread and fruit
in the kitchen—meat and fish and cold drinks in the
fridge.

Rafe handled the situation with a cool ease, Erica
noted resentfully, as though it were nothing new to him
to be married, and to a woman who obviously wished
she were anywhere but there with him. But when the
other man had left she said, engaging an equanimity that
surprised even herself, 'I take it you've been here before?'

'Yes.'

She looked at him questioningly, but he offered
nothing further, picking up their cases and taking them
upstairs.

He was in the bedroom when she followed him up a
few minutes later. A sunny room with a sea-facing
window, its sparse but serviceable furniture added to an
air of simplicity, its plain, white walls embellished with

small paintings, some of fishermen, others of local scenery.

'It normally has twin singles,' Rafe told her, as her faltering gaze came to rest on the large, calico-covered bed. 'However, as I explained to Alecco... in the circumstances...' He made a gesture with his hands, amusement curving the cruel mouth, and Erica felt the clutch of tension in her stomach from what his words and the imposing feature of the small room implied.

'Relax,' he advised drily, shrugging out of his jacket, the perfect musculature of his shoulders and chest apparent through the fine shirt. 'I'm not an inexperienced young buck impatient to discover the secrets of a woman's body. I prefer to explore the complexities of the female nature on a full stomach, suitably refreshed, and in a comfortable change of clothes.' He was reaching across the bed, throwing open one of the cases, his narrow waist and long, darkly clad legs emphasised by the hard stretch of his body. No, he was far from inexperienced, Erica thought, with a tight contraction of her stomach muscles, recalling the practised skill of his caresses in the past, the way he could still make her want him—even against her will...

'I thought you might prefer to eat out tonight, rather than rustle up something here,' she was brought out of her disconcerting thoughts to hear him suggesting. He was taking fresh clothes from the suitcase, but now he glanced up at her, eyes suddenly darkly feral, mouth pulling one side. 'Right now, I'm going to take a shower, so unless you feel like sharing one with me I suggest you stop looking at me in that dangerously provocative manner and take advantage of the bathroom and your privacy while you still have the chance.'

Blushing scarlet to realise that she'd been ogling him, she fled, seeking refuge in the bathroom and shooting the bolt home hard, the infuriating soft laughter which filtered through from the room beyond seeming to mock her lack of immunity to him, making her realise how easy it would be to ignore the warnings of her brain and let herself become ensnared by him, at least physically, as she had before.

The evening was pleasantly mild. The epitome of spring back home. Or what it was supposed to be, Erica thought wryly as they strolled down through the narrow street, because sometimes in England they seemed to miss out on spring altogether. But here that season had arrived, if not fully enough yet to warrant sunbathing, as it was still only early March, and there was a keen breeze coming off the sea that had necessitated the wearing of a warm jacket over her blouse and softly tapered white trousers. But the promise of the Mediterranean summer was there just the same, so rosy and certain in contrast to her own bleak future that she knew a moment's crushing desolation.

A sound had them turning round, and Rafe was moving sharply away from her as a small boy on a bicycle came haring through the middle of them with his feet off the pedals, his shrieks of delight making them both turn back to each other laughingly.

Rafe looked younger then, she thought, more like the man who had made her laugh and love him with a reckless adoration before, and her heart missed a beat as she saw him studying the gentle, more relaxed lines of her features. 'That's better,' he said, mouth pulling in approval, and with an odd quality to his voice. 'You know, we could really try to make something of this marriage if you'd give us half the chance.'

'You mean if I give in and condone everything you're doing to me? Forget that I was forced into it by a man I don't love?' Her voice wavered, hurt anger welling up in her from the nerve he had even to suggest it when his only reason for marrying her had been financial.

She heard him catch his breath, a sideways glance at him showing her the harsh grooves around his eyes and mouth, the tightening structure of his jaw.

'Nevertheless, we *are* married,' he emphasised, without any emotion in his voice now. 'So I suggest—for your own sake—you stop fighting me and——'

He broke off as a crashing sound and a simultaneous shriek rang out at the bottom of the hill, and before she had realised what had happened he was sprinting away from her, making no effort of the distance between himself and the boy who was now lying in a sorry heap under his bicycle, one wheel spinning fruitlessly. By the time Erica reached them, Rafe was helping the little boy to his feet.

One small hand clung trustingly to his, while the man brushed the dust off the child's clothes with almost paternal concern. But more surprisingly he was speaking to the little boy in his own language!

'He was looking at us...and not where he was going,' Rafe told her, after he had helped the boy back on to his bike and they were watching him cycle away. 'I told him to be more careful in future, but he seemed more concerned with what his mother would say about his grubby clothes than any broken bones.'

Erica couldn't restrain a smile—or her curiosity. 'And how well do you know this place, Rafe Cameron, to be able to speak to him as fluently as you obviously did in...*Greek*?'

He shrugged beneath the light, casual jacket. 'I've spent several holidays here, but the first time was with an irrigation team, and I wound up staying much longer than I'd anticipated.' Memory gave a wry curve to the firm mouth. 'You'd be surprised how much Greek one can pick up in a few months.'

She looked at him, interested, her curiosity even more aroused. But he didn't go on, and anyway they had reached the taverna, a small, local nightspot on the waterfront that Rafe had singled out for their meal.

It was dark when they came out and started the short, uphill climb back to the house. Their dinner had been pleasant, a meal of dressed lobster and salad and local wine, and Rafe had kept the conversation light—intentionally, Erica felt—so that the past hadn't intruded upon the evening. Instead, through his knowledge she learned something of the delights of Europe's first civilisation; its historic sites; the cobbled streets and chestnut forests of Lesvos and the hilly walks on Leros, as well as the quaint modes of transport, like donkeys, or caiques, if one wanted to hug the coast, or bumpy buses, where, as Rafe had smilingly explained to her, 'livestock occasionally hop on for a free ride.'

She had laughed with him—despite herself—at that, while from a corner of the friendly, thatched taverna, the rhythmic strings of a bouzouki had filled the night with song.

Now a full, high moon shone gently on the whitewashed houses. Lights winked at them from one of the smaller islands across the bay, and from somewhere above them in the night-scented forest the breeze brought with it the pungent fragrance of pine.

A night perfect for romance. For seduction...

'Are you cold?' Her sudden, involuntary shiver brought Rafe's arm around her, tightening, when she would have pulled away. 'No... stay here.'

His body was warm—too warm—and disturbingly male, the proud silhouette of his features giving rise to the fancy of some ancient Greek god: eloquent, powerful, physically perfect. Most women would probably have given anything to have changed places with her at that moment, she realised, with a sudden, reckless longing for what might have been, his nearness, the scent of his cologne so insidiously stimulating to her that she knew a chilling fear for her own immunity.

When they reached the house, she would have made for the kitchen under the pretext of wanting a nightcap if that strong arm hadn't been so relentlessly determined to keep her with him, guiding her towards the bedroom.

He left her standing trembling beside the door-jamb to switch on the light beside the bed, its pink rays throwing a warm blush over the coverlet. Then he was tossing his jacket aside, unbuttoning his shirt.

'Come here.'

Erica steeled herself, a small pulse beating furiously at her throat, the rush of blood through her veins so enervating that she moved across the room to him on legs that felt decidedly boneless.

He took a moment to study her—the soft oval of her face, the patrician nose that lent her that sophisticated air she was far from aware of, the full, wide mouth— and very gently he lifted a hand to the soft coil at the nape of her neck, bringing her hair cascading down around her shoulders in a golden wave. Lightly, his fingers trailed along the delicate structure of her jaw, moving with a heart-stopping deliberation down the smooth column of her throat where he brought both hands into play to slip her jacket off her shoulders. Casually, he tossed it on to the chair with his, his movements easy and unflustered, so at variance with the tension in her own body—the sudden, rapid pounding of her heart.

Gaze riveted on his bared chest—that pyramid of crisp, dark hair tapering down and disappearing below his belt—she sucked in her breath as he began unfastening her blouse, every nerve taut as a bow-string. She closed her eyes, and, feeling the cool air from the open window on her skin, was disconcerted to realise that the fabric had fallen open, leaving the lace-covered swell of her breasts exposed.

'I hate you.' She drew the words through gritted teeth, her breathing rapid, shallow.

'I know.' His voice was soft, yet oddly hoarse, and when he made no move to touch her she opened her eyes, meeting a dark emotion she couldn't make out in his. 'Still...' His smile was suddenly cruel. 'Neither of us made any undying promises of love, did we?' he reminded her, and with a return of such scathing cynicism that she drew back with a small shudder, rebellion masking the bitter injury in her eyes.

He looked at her obliquely, one black eyebrow arched. 'Are you trying to tell me you want to rescind the terms of our agreement?'

Her heart seemed to stand still as his hand cupped the full roundness of her breast, the caressing action of his thumb across the lacy bra sending a shock like electricity tingling through her. She swallowed, wishing she could say yes, but knowing her father would be the one to suffer if she did. She could smell the potent warmth of him, nostrils flaring with the musky scent of his skin beneath the gaping shirt. Nevertheless, holding on to some composure in spite of what he was doing to her, she lifted her small chin to say caustically, 'What agreement? The truth—in exchange for my body?'

The hard light in his eyes was swiftly obliterated by the thick sweep of his lashes. 'If it were just your body I wanted, I would have made you my mistress—not my wife.'

His cold self-assurance made her lips compress in angry mutiny, her gaze drawn unwittingly to the heavy lifting of that muscular chest. 'No, you wanted it all, didn't you?' Heatedly, she was throwing back. 'To own a piece of Witneys—me! Well if you think that forcing me to marry you—ruining *my* life is likely to make me respect you,' she spat, battling against a merciless anguish that threatened to show through the barriers of her defence, 'you're wrong—because it won't!'

Momentarily, Rafe's face darkened, then that cynical smile curved his lips. 'How naïve you still are, my sweet,' he said, infuriatingly softly, the back of his hand cool—disturbingly sensual—against her cheek. 'I don't intend being satisfied with a mere piece of Witneys—I intend to *be* Witneys—and quite honestly I don't give a damn what you feel about me. But if you're trying to tell me you'd rather have the obsequious Caddis for a husband, then your taste is as poor as your judgement, and one day, Erica, you may even thank me for rescuing you from a social-climbing groveller such as he is. He might have convinced himself he was in love with you—might even have married you eventually. But do you really think his interest in you personally would ever be greater than what you could do for his career?'

So he still believed she was in love with Graham. Well, she wasn't going to disillusion him! she thought tartly, about to retort that he was no better himself. But a finger was against her lips. 'And since you've obviously made up your mind as to your status where I'm concerned, dearest...' he looked strangely weary, his tone half amused, half bored '...may I point out that possessions don't answer back?'

She would have lashed out at him then, but strong arms had taken control, pulling her down on to the yielding softness of the bed, so that somehow she was lying across his lap, her panicky protest stifled beneath the sudden, bruising pressure of his mouth.

She was sinking down under a sea of bitter-sweet oblivion, trying desperately to stay afloat, the feel of his hands on her body as they rediscovered its smooth curvature a pleasure it knew and welcomed, even as her mind rejected it. He was tugging at the front fastening of her bra, releasing it, and she caught her breath as his hands moved up to knead the soft flesh it had uncovered.

'Rafe, no...'

It was a tremulous objection, and futile, because he took no heed of it, his lips following the pleasurable journey of his hands to close over each proud tumescent peak in turn.

The familiar strength of him against her dragged a small cry from her lips, the sight of his dark head against her breast with the suckling warmth of his mouth sending such an acute ache of need piercing through her that she had to grit her teeth against it.

She had longed for this! she acknowledged with a soul-shattering, shaming admission. Wanted him—in spite of everything—for all the lonely days and nights since he had first awakened her to the ecstasy of his caresses, so that no other man could ever quite match up to him. But he must never know that. Never! Her self-respect surfaced even while she acknowledged that she was his to do with as he liked, that that was the price she had paid for her father's freedom from disgrace—an enslaving of herself to a man who felt only contempt for her.

The thought helped to cool her ardour, so that, as he removed the rest of her clothes, with a cold, impassive resignation she let him do it. But when he shed his own and came down on her, she had to stifle a gasp from the sudden shock of his warm nakedness—the coarseness of his body hair against her soft flesh—praying he wouldn't guess how hoplessly he aroused her.

But, of course, he knew. He was too skilled a lover not to recognise the signs—that sensual flush across her skin, her eagerly responding breasts—his lips moving with a slow deliberation down over her ribcage, burning a hot, lingering trail over the ivory plane of her abdomen and the long, dark line that marred it.

She felt his hesitation and tensed, even before she heard his deep voice enquire, 'Why the scar?'

Of course, he hadn't been aware of it before, she remembered, her shyness with him, with the high-briefed bikinis she had worn that summer, keeping the evidence of that cruel operation from being disclosed.

Hazily—shakily—she heard herself murmuring something about appendicitis, realising with a trembling relief that that had satisfied him when she felt his tongue move caressingly along the long line of scar tissue, stimulating and warm.

Oh, dear heaven! How could she bear it? His coaxing seduction was almost too much for her to take, her moment's dread that he might somehow have guessed the truth shaking her resistance so much that she was very much in danger now of surrendering to the sudden, breath-catching intimacy of his mouth—his hands—her whole body tingling from the effort not to arch invitingly against him, to draw him up to her, run her hands over that broad back and caress the rippling silk of his skin. When suddenly he moved, though, one knee parting her thighs, she let out a small protest, tensing in total rejection.

'Relax, Erica.' He was aware, of course, of how she was feeling, just as he was aware, too, that she was ready for him, even if she was fighting him with every shred of her fruitless will. She sensed his holding back, then heard his agonised groan as he lost control, his driving energies all but taking her with him, while she lay tottering on the brink of some gaping chasm that promised ecstasy and fulfilment, and afterwards such utter, utter humiliation...

She clamped her teeth over her lower lip, closing her senses to her wildly pounding heart—his shuddering groan of release—only daring to move when eventually he withdrew, turning away from him on to her side, knowing the strongest feeling of defeat and a physical frustration such as she had never known.

'You silly little fool.' Rafe's voice penetrated the dim stillness that surrounded them, reprehending—quietly angry. 'It would have been so much better for you if you'd just let go and taken what you wanted. But no, you had to salve that stubborn pride of yours, didn't you?' Her breath locked in her lungs as his hand ran down the curve of her waist and rested against her hip, and he said in a curiously husky voice, 'Are you all right?'

She felt unsated desire tremble through her at his touch—wanting, as she had never wanted anything—but the pride he had accused her of had her pulling away from him without a word, and after a few moments she heard him get out of bed and go downstairs.

When she awoke, the sun was streaming in through the lace-curtained window. She moved cautiously, a covert glance at the other half of the bed showing it to be unoccupied, only the indentation on the pillow assuring her that she hadn't dreamt last night. That, and a few tender spots on her body from where Rafe had made her his.

Warm colour invaded her cheeks from the memory of his kisses, the pleasurable agony of his possession that she had fought to resist. For hours last night, after Rafe had come quietly back to bed without disturbing her—obviously thinking she was asleep—she had lain there, wondering how she could be so stupid as to imagine she could hold out for any length of time against such an assault on her senses in the way she had last night, to permit his lovemaking without giving in to the restless needs that racked her own body. He might have demanded this marriage purely for his own ends, but she had agreed to it for her father's sake. And, whether she let Rafe take her in passive acceptance or in a storm of mutual passion, the outcome would be the same...

Then why shouldn't she just give in? Accept the inevitable? She was shocked to find herself considering, pulling up her thoughts right there, ashamed that she had even entertained them. Because he blackmailed you into marrying him, a little voice reminded her with cold, unyielding logic. Don't pride yourself he has even the slightest scrap of feeling for you personally.

Well, the feeling—or lack of it—was mutual! she thought, with a burning fervency which held no conviction, which was merely a shield against the hollow emptiness she was suddenly experiencing deep down inside. Oh, goodness! She couldn't let her emotions fall victim to him a second time. She couldn't!

Footsteps outside her door had her making a swift grab for the sheet, just as Rafe came in with a breakfast tray. His mouth quirked at the prim little gesture, which she knew must have seemed ludicrous after what had happened last night, but he didn't make any comment, saying simply as he set the tray down on the bedside cabinet, 'I thought you might like to see around the island, so I've arranged for a boat. Eat up like a good girl and come down as soon as you can. I'll get a picnic lunch together.'

His offer surprised her, as did his abrupt departure. She had imagined enduring yet a further ravaging of her senses this morning and was relieved for her sanity's sake that he was abandoning desire for sightseeing, although she couldn't help—understand—an illogical little feeling of hurt pride in realising how easily he could do without her.

The day proved pleasanter than she had imagined. The boat Rafe had hired was a small cruiser which he handled as if he cruised every day, and as the vessel cut through the sparkling water he pointed out the varying coastlines of other islands.

The black, volcanic shingle of one, she noticed, changed, with another, to dense pine forests stretching right down to the water's edge. White, cube-shaped houses and sleepy hotels boasted of what, in summer, would be busy resorts, the dark hills above them tumbling away to secluded bays for the more peace-loving tourist. The pinks, red and yellows of early spring flowers spread vivid colours across the lush slopes, and ever-present were the vineyards, citrus orchards and silver-leafed olive-groves, all flourishing under a sky that gave its brilliance to the glittering blue sea.

They picnicked on the boat, mooring in a quiet bay, and afterwards, when Rafe brought the cruiser in and suggested a walk, Erica readily agreed.

The hand that helped her on to dry land was warm and strong, bringing her into startlingly close proximity with his hard body. Remembering last night, she felt an unwelcome *frisson* shoot through her, and she pulled away, tugging off her shoes and running with sudden, feverish abandon into the sea. It was cold, and she gasped with the shock of it, kicking at the waves that hissed over her slender ankles, giving vent to her frustrations.

'Who are you angry with?'

Rafe had joined her, his own shoes discarded, the contact she had wanted to avoid now a possessive arc around her shoulders.

'Do I have to be angry with anyone?' she said pointedly, disconcerted that he could assess her feelings so well, because she was angry, at herself—if no one else—for wanting him still.

He gave her a lop-sided smile, a flash of white against the olive skin. 'Kicking out like that I'd say you were very, very angry.'

She laughed without humour, and this time when she tried to pull away found herself caught mercilessly against the rough warmth of his sweater.

'What have you been doing for the past five years, Erica? Breaking hearts? Is there a string of young men all over London—and Europe,' he interposed drily, 'bruised for life for falling for that unpitying loveliness of yours?'

His tongue flayed, but she looked at him with a proud lift of her head, meeting eyes that were clear, half hooded by heavy lids. If *he* had been bruised, then his wounds had healed long ago, she realised, anguished, her features held in tight restraint as she glanced out across the sparkling sea.

'That's right,' she bluffed, her tone cool, yet tinged with acidity. 'Well, what else would you expect from daddy's little socialite? I had to amuse myself somehow. Fast cars and casinos lose their attraction after a while. At least, with men, there's always a new face—a new personality. It helps relieve the boredom for some of the time.'

Well, wasn't that what he wanted to hear? she thought bitterly, and, feeling the way that masculine chest expanded, wondered why.

'Myrtle said you'd got a degree.'

Of course. And it had shocked him, she reflected, managing to extricate herself from him now, feeling her attempt to keep him from seeing through the hard veneer to the real Erica Witney wearing rather thin.

'I was a lucky student,' she purported, stuffing her hands into the pockets of the anorak she had worn on the boat because the breeze had been keen off-shore—wading with him through the cool water. 'Some couldn't mix business and pleasure—I found it easy. There was really nothing clever about that.'

'You were also a virgin,' he reminded her, with sudden, cruel blatancy, 'and we both know that normally you aren't exactly the frigid type when you're in a man's arms.'

Only those razor-sharp reflexes stopped her hand from reaching its target, his tugging hers down as he surveyed the hot, angry colour in her cheeks.

'I was just making a point,' he commented, in more conciliatory tones, a frown knitting his brows, hard grooves etching themselves around the strong mouth and jaw. 'All I can say is you must have worked darned hard to have kept from falling into the temptations of early involvement which is all too easy for most young people. I also know Sir Joshua's too shrewd to let any department of his company suffer for the sake of nepotism—even if it is his beloved daughter—especially when there must have been scores of well-qualified executives just waiting for the chance to step into the position you've managed to secure.' He let go of her arm, and his voice was suddenly scathing against the gentle wash of the sea. 'What happened, Erica? Get fed up with the good life that quickly?' She caught her breath, feeling his disparaging remark like the brush of nettles across her skin. She couldn't tell him that there hadn't been anyone through a lack of opportunity, but because no one else had come even remotely near to stirring her emotionally, or physically, since she had broken up with him. Nor could she tell him that the reason she had worked so hard was to try and drive him from her mind, forget his brutal infidelity, his accusations when she hadn't agreed to marry him—the thing she'd wanted most in the world and couldn't have because Nature had been so cruel . . .

So she said, with a careless little shrug, 'Something like that,' keeping her eyes trained on the pine-clad horizon so that he wouldn't see what was in them. 'Anyway,' she went on, her voice suddenly defensive, 'you haven't exactly been living a monk's life yourself, have you?' Whenever she had seen pictures of him in the newspapers, he was usually with some beautiful woman. She recalled one in particular who had appeared with him regularly enough for the Press to start publishing rumours of a serious romance between them, and, reminding him, she added with rather forced indifference, 'She was mature and very glamorous—just your type, I would have thought. I must admit I was rather surprised when nothing came of that.' And that wasn't all she'd felt, reluctantly she admitted to herself now, because she'd known relief, too—a release of such illogical, gutrotting emotions that she'd been almost sick.

'Are you?' he grimaced, walking on again, the dark hair, blown untidily by the wind, adding something to that raw, masculine attraction. 'Well, some people will print anything if they think it will sell newspapers, and my work with that lady was purely a promotional thing. She also happened to have a husband somewhere around, and, contrary to what you've always wanted to think, Erica, married women have never been my scene.'

'No?' she sneered, her heart seeming to twist inside her, pain prompting her to add with cutting contention, 'And I suppose Laverne just happened to *throw* herself into your arms!'

'That's about the size of it.' His swift declaration brought her gaze startlingly to his, and the firm mouth pulled down grimly when he saw the wounded scepticism mirrored there. 'Your stepmother had...problems,' he stated tersely. 'Oh, she was a very desirable woman, but hardly worth cheating on a man I liked and respected—or risking jeopardising my...prospects with you. On that account, of course, I needn't have worried, need I?'

That last, cutting comment clearly reinforced his opinion of her, and imperceptibly she shivered. But what he'd said about Laverne—about liking and respecting her father—threw her mental processes into confusion and she turned sharply away from those penetrating eyes, wanting—incredibly!—to believe him. Dear heaven! In spite of everything, she wanted him to be telling the truth, she realised, afraid, her toes curling tensely into the cool sand of the sea-bed as she wrestled with her startled thoughts. Was it possible that she had been wrong about him all these years, just as he'd been wrong about her? Because for the first time it struck her that what she'd thought was an intimate clinch between him and Laverne when she'd walked in on them that night could have been an act of rejection on Rafe's part, those strong hands clutching her stepmother not embracing her but holding her at bay—the emotion on his face one of anger and not passion as she'd immediately assumed. She looked up, her attention caught by a solitary hang-glider way above them, rising and dipping on the warm air currents, wings spread like a huge, predatory bird. Was that what he had been trying to tell her when she had refused to listen? Had he been in love with *her*—faithful to her—all along? Or had he simply been angry at the thought of losing her because of the prospects he'd just openly admitted he hadn't wanted to jeopardise, which marrying her had obviously held in store for him?

Embroiled in her tormented thoughts, she started as Rafe's arm shot across her middle, stopping her in her tracks.

'Tread on that and it wouldn't be very pleasant,' he assured her about the little black spiky ball she could see now, distorted by the rippling of the water. She was trembling, not from narrowly escaping those protective spines, but because of the warm hand splayed across her abdomen, holding her with a myriad sensations that only intensified when she looked up into the strong, hard beauty of his features.

'It wouldn't have been much fun for the sea-urchin either,' she declared, her nervous little laugh breaking the dangerous spell he seemed to be weaving around her.

'Still the sworn animal lover, Erica?'

His tone mocked, although his smile was indulgent as he steered her back to the safety of the beach, and she recalled that look, that evening at that barbecue such an eternity ago, when she had been arguing her case for animal rights. He had been on her side that night, she remembered in spite of herself, surprisingly defending her views, filling her adolescent heart with a deep and innocent admiration for him until he'd taught her the meaning of real love—passion...

Stupidly, she felt tears bite behind her eyes, was suddenly startled to realise that she was still in as much danger from him emotionally as she had ever been, and, looking away from him, in a voice tremulous from her discovery, she murmured, 'Let's go back now, shall we?'

They had dinner with Alecco and his family. Maria Stavros was a plump, friendly woman who added a homeliness to her simple yet cosy little house. A young Greek beauty with long black hair and laughing eyes, a year or two older than Erica, was introduced to her as Alecco's niece.

'Vikki is a nurse...and a very good one,' he said proudly, his dark face cracking in a broad grin. 'When your husband is badly sick...she take care.'

Erica smiled and sent a questioning glance in Rafe's direction. She was having difficulty understanding Alecco's English.

'He's referring to the time I had an argument with a ton of rubble and broke more bones than I realised I had,' Rafe told her with a grimace. 'Vikki very kindly nursed me back to shape again.'

'I see.' A guarded glance at the Greek girl who had very boldly perched herself on the arm of his chair assured Erica that Vikki Stavros had enjoyed the task immensely. The bright smile she flashed at Rafe was more than one of just admiration for an attractive male she had nursed.

'What he *didn't* tell you,' the girl enlarged, clearly pleased to be hugging a confidence that even his wife didn't share, 'is that he did it checking the safety of an underground channel he wasn't happy with, before he allowed his men to start work there.' Vikki's English— unlike Alecco's and Maria's—was perfect, as was the rather too well structured face and figure, Erica thought astringently, irked by the way the girl's arm rested on the back of Rafe's chair so that one unpainted but beautifully manicured hand was just touching his shoulder, one bare brown leg, drawn up under the full, tight-waisted skirt, angled towards him with a body language that spoke volumes. 'His instincts were right. It wasn't safe. Consequently, no one but Rafe was hurt, but the casualties could have been...' She threw out her hands, not needing to finish. 'You wouldn't believe the respect this man commands, and because of it he's got a great team. Did you know he's been responsible for a lot of the irrigation on this island... and that his work has benefited people in the Third World as well?' She sent him an adoring look and, as she inclined her head, long raven hair almost brushed his cheek. 'He's really quite a guy.'

And you're really quite smitten! Erica thought, rather bitchily, before Rafe's deep voice cut across her thoughts.

'I think you've said quite enough, sweetheart,' she was surprised to hear him addressing the other girl—not at all embarrassed by her over-zealous little speech, although she detected a mild chiding in the Scottish, male tones. 'Carry on like that and you could well destroy the illusion of the total brute my wife likes to think she married.'

Everyone laughed, thinking it a joke. Why shouldn't they? Erica thought unhappily, pretending to share their humour, although when her eyes met Rafe's she tensed, seeing only cool mockery in their sapphire depths. He got up then with that lithe grace of his, moving to look at some carpentry Alecco wanted to show him—his tall, lean physique superb beside the portly Greek's—and Erica breathed relief as they went outside, more affected than she wanted to admit by what the other girl had told her. Strangely, though, she wasn't that surprised. She knew Rafe well enough to know that he wasn't a man to pass the buck or to expect anyone to do what he wouldn't be prepared to do himself. Wasn't that just one of the reasons she'd admired him—fallen in love with him in the beginning? And perhaps if she'd shown more interest in his work he might have given her some insight into it himself, she reflected, with a reluctant revival of that former respect for him—but she hadn't, curious though she had been, not wanting him to think that she was weakening towards him, condoning this marriage he had forced upon her.

Suddenly Vikki was asking her what she thought of the island, suprisingly, unexpectedly friendly. Then a little later the two men returned, and a steaming pie was brought in, served with piping hot vegetables which, Erica discovered, tasted as delicious as it looked. Afterwards there was ouzo, and Alecco acquainted Erica with some of the islands' legends, while Vikki translated as Maria advised Erica of all she should try to see while she was there, until Rafe suggested it was time they left.

'Of course, we keep them too long.' Alecco gave a meaningful smile. 'I forgot we have an anxious bride-groom here, eager for his bride.'

Rafe made some deep, amused comment in Greek, that raw, fervid light in his eyes as they clashed with Erica's drying her throat from that familiar, unwelcome excitement so that she could have kicked herself for blushing. At the door, she was aware of Vikki reaching up to kiss Rafe fully on the lips, and couldn't help the hot surge of emotion she felt as the girl stepped back from him, her face aglow. With a coiling anguish in her stomach, she wondered if he and Vikki had been lovers.

'Quite convenient coming here for a honeymoon, wasn't it?' her overstretched emotions urged her into saying as they were walking back. 'If your wife doesn't come up with all you expect of her, someone else will!'

One sudden movement from him jerked her to a halt, and she was staring up into eyes that were glittering with anger. 'Vikki is a very dear friend,' he told her, his voice cold in its defence of the Mediterranean beauty. 'As are Alecco and Maria.' Suddenly, his anger was ebbing, re-placed by a coolly mocking smile. 'If I didn't know you better, sweetheart, I'd have to admit to believing that you're just a little bit jealous.'

'*Jealous?*' she spat incredulously, refusing to ac-knowledge the emotion that burned hotly and ir-rationally within her. 'Do you really think I care if another woman wants to drape herself all over you? As far as I'm concerned she can have you, and your precious irrigation programmes! I'm sure you'll both make her very happy! And at least to take *her* to bed you won't have to stoop to emotional blackmail!'

His face was a dark profile against the moon as she tore away from him with a sob in her threat. She thought he'd come after her—retaliate in some way—but he didn't, and she had to pay for her childish outbursts by having to wait for him when she reached the house because she didn't have a key.

Yes, she was jealous, she admitted hopelessly to herself now. But why? Why, when all she was to him was a means of securing some satisfactory financial liaison with her father? When she knew he despised her so much?

'Erica...' He moved into the shadows of the porch, the disturbing scent of him such torture to her senses above the delicate perfume of a shrub that climbed the sun-soaked walls. 'Erica you should know there's only one woman I intend to take to bed...to make love to.'

He let her into the house, the sound of the door closing behind them bringing home to her the enshrouding intimacy of the place, and tensely, on a rather tremulous note, she said, 'Why? Because you want to control me as you're planning to control my father's company?'

In shadow, the broad shoulders squared, then relaxed, and suddenly he was reaching for her, all her powers of resistance leaping to defend her from her own traitorous longing to be crushed against him as he pulled her into his arms.

'Yes,' he breathed on a hard, ragged note. 'To control you. To own you. To make you pregnant. Because only the thought of my child inside you gives me any peace. Only the thought of you beneath me, sobbing, pleading, because of what I'm doing to you...'

His mouth was on hers, demanding the response she was fighting to keep from him, his arms pulling her hard against him so that she could feel the full evidence of his arousal. His strength—his warmth—was turning her bones to liquid fire and she was clinging to him for support, her body arching into his of its own volition as her lips suddenly parted in answering abandon to his kiss.

She was responding to his urgent mouth with a desperation long born of hopelessness, wanting this to go on and on, and she gave a small groan of protest when he lifted his head, using his shoulder as a shield against the betraying emotions that ravaged her.

'No,' he said raggedly—determinedly. 'You'll face it.' He lifted her chin with cruel fingers, cruel as the scrutiny with which he surveyed her vulnerable features. 'You want me...here. Now. Though you'll never admit it, will you? But may I remind you, my sweet Erica, that there was a time when you were begging me for this?'

She winced from the reminder, giving a small cry as he swept her up into his arms, carrying her up the stairs as if she were weightless. When he placed her down on the bed, she began to struggle, making it harder for him to remove her clothes, though he did so with enough ease to make mockery of her efforts to stop him. He laughed softly when she lay naked beneath him, and she felt the absence of his own clothes like fire to her already fevered skin. He was gentle then, his lips anointing her body with such unbelievable tenderness that reality became a blur, her being only alive to the world of touch and sensation and exquisite pleasure he was creating for her until, without realising it, she cried out to him for the fulfilment and the release only he could give her. And this time when he took her there was no question of her resisting him, and no pain, her own need driving her into an instant and shattering crescendo of desire that tore shuddering sobs from her throat. And a long time afterwards when she lay silent, facing away from him, through her chastening humiliation she heard him say, 'Don't feel so bad about it, my sweet.' His tone was grazing and cold. 'If you really need something to justify abandoning yourself to me like that...you can always blame the wine.'

CHAPTER FOUR

THEY returned to England to a grey, interminable drizzle. Having put her own flat up for sale, Erica spent the first couple of days moving various belongings into Rafe's luxurious penthouse where he had decided they would live. It was a huge, airy apartment overlooking the Thames, the windows of the spacious lounge opening on to balconies and breathtaking views of the city. One mirrored wall reflected a room superlative in its décor, a thick, creamy carpet and matching velvet curtains blending perfectly with the low, and very expensive-looking suite. Well-sculpted marble lamps graced handmade occasional tables, while bookshelves bulged with knowledge and lighter reading material, the paintings around the walls tasteful and obviously original.

It lacked life, though, Erica decided, as soon as she stepped inside, and that very day after Rafe had gone to work set about filling it with several, more homely touches: extra cushions, a few small ornaments, and plants—dozens of them. Some were new, but most she had already transferred personally from her own home—not trusting them to the removal-men—begonias, cyclamens and various ferns, including a flamboyant thing with exotic, creamy flowers in an equally exotic pot, which she put on the shelf above the impressive hi-fi system, and which she treasured.

Consequently, when Rafe came home, the unexpected sight of all the foliage that had suddenly appeared in his absence had him exclaiming, 'Good grief! It looks like an arboretum!'

'Don't you like it?' She laid aside the little red plant-waterer she'd been using, looking rather dismayed. 'You said I could bring anything I liked from home...'

Mouth twisting in amusement, he sent another look around him, hands embracing the room. 'All of these came out of that little flat?'

'Yes, and—careful!' she exhaled, because he had just tossed a newspaper down on to the hi-fi cabinet, causing the leaves of her prized specimen to shudder in objection. 'That one's rare and very delicate, and it doesn't like direct sunlight so it couldn't go anywhere else.'

'It also needs careful watering, hates draughts and thrives best with regular feeding.' A curious smile curved his lips. And softly, 'I know. I bought it for you.'

Disconcerted that he should have remembered, she swung away from him to finish watering the rest, trying to conceal her inner tension as he continued to harp on the point. 'I'm surprised you still have it. I would have thought that would have been one of the first things in the bin.'

Perhaps it should have been, she thought, hair falling like a golden curtain as she tended to another little plant, her movements controlled and deliberate, refusing to rise to the bait, though she knew exactly what he must be thinking. That it was odd how something he had given her should still mean so much to her, and she really couldn't explain to herself, let alone him, why she had kept it—nurtured it. Perhaps it was because it represented something she would never have from him again—something given with love, something living...

Long lashes concealing any emotion, she straightened, giving a little gasp as she stepped back against him, unaware that he'd been right behind her.

'Aren't you going to give me a kiss?' He turned her round in his arms, so that her hands flew up in a self-protective gesture against his shoulders, water spilling out of the tiny plastic vessel on to the carpet.

'Why?' she queried tersely, turning her head away, brows drawn together from the effort of trying to ignore the sudden stirring warmth of his hard body, that musky male scent of him beneath the superbly tailored beige suit intensified by a long day in the office. 'I'm sure if you want one, you'll take it.'

He laughed, a soft sound against that of a boat's resonant horn way below on the river. 'Is that what you want?' His lips brushed the sensitive hollow where her neck met her shoulder, teasing beneath the open blouse she wore under the dark dungarees, causing her breath to lock painfully in her lungs. 'Do you get some warped kind of kick out of pretending to yourself that I always take you by force?'

She stiffened in resistance, unable to say anything, knowing as well as he did that that was all a denial would be—pretence. But she must be sick, she thought—struggling to resist the shuddering effects of his mouth on her skin—to welcome the caresses of a man who had forced her into marrying him, giving herself in hopeless, humiliating surrender to him night after night. Because she had long given up trying to fight him. The physical chemistry between them was too strong—an irresistible pull of two forces that, when he took her to bed, caused such chaos to her senses that she became nothing but a mindless marionette to his will. But it was a purely physical thing, she assured herself as she had over and over again—afraid and ashamed to admit that it might be anything deeper and more complex—and now that shame had her pushing at him in an attempt to free herself.

'Rafe...' Her voice trembled while she tried to hold him at bay. 'I want to talk to you... about Dad.'

'What about him?' His voice, as he pulled her against him again, was deep and oddly hoarse, his breath against the small, pink curve of her ear sending unbearably pleasurable tingles down her spine.

'You promised,' she reminded him firmly, holding him back, her gaze lucid and steady as she looked up into the dark, hooded depths of his. 'We made a bargain,' she stressed, her heartbeat a debilitating thud from having to broach the subject, 'that if I married you... you'd help him... supply that evidence. Well?' she prompted, swallowing, her demand tremulous for all the challenge it contained.

'Well what?' he queried, with infuriating mock ignorance so that rather nervously she was forced to spell it out.

'Are you going to help him?' Her head was at an angle, eyes scanning the hard, superb symmetry of his face. 'Don't you think you should ring his solicitor—tell him that you know he's innocent—that you can clear his name?'

His mouth moved wryly. 'And let you get away?' Amusement laced his words, but she could see from his eyes that he was deadly serious, panic rising in her as he swung away, picked up his newspaper and flopped carelessly down into a chair.

'You promised!' she exhaled again, unable to believe that he was still holding out, and now angry tears were smarting behind her eyes. 'You've gone back on your word. You said if I agreed to marry you, you'd turn over that evidence. Well I have married you! And it certainly wasn't for the pleasure of your company!'

He looked at her from over the top of his paper, a black eyebrow arching at her angry outburst. Clearly, though, he had no intention of joining her in a shouting

match, because he said quietly, his voice level and controlled, 'We're both well aware of that, dearest. And
regardless of what you'd like to think, I haven't gone
back on my word. I've never set a definite date for producing those papers, if you remember, and no business-
man commits his securities to another party without first
having some indemnity in return.'

'What do you mean?' she quizzed warily, her knuckles
white against the hard, red plastic of the plant-waterer
as her worst fears began to take positive shape. 'You've
got the marriage licence!'

'Which is worth about as much as the ink it's written
with—and you know it,' he stated decisively. 'Oh, come
on, darling...' Casually, he folded his paper, tossing it
down on to the coffee-table, sitting back again with an
easy demeanour that had Erica far from fooled. Like a
beautiful beast of the jungle he never really let go, that
guarded watchfulness and sharp sagacity ever present,
even at his most relaxed. 'You know as well as I do that
if I don't protect my own interests the moment I give
you what you married me for this partnership will be
about as dead and finished as last Tuesday!' The hard
mouth firmed. 'Naturally, I have to take adequate
measures to ensure that we both benefit from
our...arrangement, Erica, and I do believe I mentioned
that children were also part of the deal. You knew it—
and agreed to it. Therefore, sweetheart, I don't think it's
too unreasonable for you to expect me to hang fire for
a while, so ask me again when you're pregnant.'

'You——!' She bit back the distasteful adjective,
fingers tightening on the plant-waterer to stop herself
hurling it straight at him as casually he got to his feet.

And he must have read her mind, because with a lop-
sided pull of his lips he was advising, 'And if you're
thinking of throwing that, may I recommend that you
empty it out first? Much as I need a shower I prefer to

get undressed beforehand, and, while I rather relish a tussle with you, my sweet, I think it only fair to remind you that I have the advantage on my side.'

Which was a very subtle and clever way of keeping her under control, she realised, staring broodily after his broad back as he went out of the room, because the thought of provoking him into actual, angry physical combat with her where she would only come off worst, and probably very humiliated, helped cool her temper considerably.

She couldn't comprehend, though, how he could still refuse to help her father, the further condition he was imposing before he agreed to sending little needles of anxiety threading through her with cruel, piercing tips. Of course, he wasn't stupid. He knew that as soon as he produced that evidence he'd have no hold over her, and he couldn't risk losing that. While she was his wife, Witneys was as good as in his pocket, and that, she accepted, stifling the choking sob that came up in her throat, was all he really wanted. But when she failed to produce the child he seemed so bent on extracting from her, what then? she wondered chillingly. He would see to it that she took those fertility tests, and when he learned the results he'd be so angry, more likely than not he'd refuse to speak up for her father because she'd been so dishonest with him, and where would Sir Joshua be then? The legal proceedings were dragging on and on, and, if he didn't eventually wind up in prison, then at the very least, without Rafe's help, his reputation would be blighted for life. What life he could enjoy, she thought unhappily—worriedly—because she doubted whether his health could stand the strain of something like that hanging over him forever. And then as well, when Rafe discovered the truth about her—that marrying her was preventing him from ever having the children he wanted—he would, of course, leave her.

She couldn't comprehend the savage twist of pain she experienced on arriving at that very understandable deduction. Wasn't that what she really wanted? To be free from the shackles he'd put around her? Free from his contempt over what he'd believed about her in the past?

Well, of course it was! she thought fiercely, but without really convincing herself, because ever since that day when he'd told her about Laverne, she had known intuitively that he was telling the truth, and she was coming dangerously close to being in love with him again. Ever since then, half of her had ached to tell him that he'd been wrong about her, too, all those years ago— that really she had looked up to him, admired him, with all the awe-inspired adulation of her seventeen years. But she had her pride, and common sense told her that, whatever he had felt about her in the past, he certainly wasn't in love with her now. And anyway, if she told him he'd been wrong about her, she'd also have to tell him why she hadn't accepted his proposal before, and she had to keep him from knowing that—for her father's sake. She could only hope she could change his mind about withholding that evidence before he found out the truth.

Life wasn't made any easier in the office when, on her return, she was met by a barrage of comments and congratulations, particularly from some of the female staff who wanted to know how it felt to have hooked a man as virile and dynamic as Rafe Cameron. With a mask of cordiality that hid the misery in her eyes, Erica simply smiled at their envying remarks, giving away nothing of her inner emotions. Graham still continued to avoid her, until he was forced, purely through the execution of his duties one afternoon, to come into her office, and then he only reiterated what he had said the day after he had called round to her flat and found her with Rafe.

'You didn't breathe a word to me that you were seeing him when we were in court that day, did you?' he accused, obviously taking their break-up far harder than she'd hoped. 'Well, I can only say that it's all a bit sudden,' he commented, with his mouth twisting unpleasantly. 'I don't suppose you realise that there's gossip going round this building as to why you got married in such a rush?'

He was strutting round the office looking like a small boy who hadn't got what he wanted. Which wasn't strictly true, because he had got that promotion, and without her help, Erica throught wryly, staring at his typically executive-looking striped tie. And if the rest of the office had preconceived ideas about her hasty marriage to Rafe, then they would soon be proved wrong, she considered grievously, hurt as much by that as the fact that everyone must be thinking she was deliriously happy. How doubly wrong they all were! she thought, with a poignant stab of anguish somewhere around her heart.

Over the following days, however, she came to a decision. That it was pointless carrying on a cold war or hurling abuse at Rafe if she wanted to get that vital evidence out of him. If he'd loved her at all, he must have been hurt profoundly by the things he'd let himself believe about her, she reasoned torturedly, so that if all he wanted to do was hurt her now, she couldn't wholly blame him. Surely, then, wasn't it up to her to show him that she wasn't the supercilious creature he believed her to be? Be more civil to him and at least try to win back his respect, if not his love? she mused, torn by the knowledge that if she had killed that love through her own weakness—her inability to be completely honest with him five years ago—she had no one to blame but herself. Certainly, it would have been better to have lost him through the truth—still having his respect—instead of concealing it in the way she had and having to endure his total contempt for her now, she realised in retrospect, determined to change his opinion of her if it was the last thing she did.

'What's all this?' half amused, he wanted to know one Saturday morning, noticing the red rose in the centre of the breakfast table from a bouquet he had bought her earlier in the week.

'I thought the table needed a bit of colour,' she lied, hoping she hadn't gone over the top, a flush creeping up her throat above the lace-edged satin négligé she wore.

'Very decorative,' he said softly, sitting down, those blue eyes taking in both the bloom and Erica in one appreciative male embrace that, against her will, made her stomach flip, along with the fresh vitality of his appearance.

He had teamed dark denim jeans with a dark blue shirt, the open neck of which revealed the crisp hair that curled beneath the dark strength of his throat, while the soft cotton hugging the broad shoulders and tapering waist was unable to conceal the perfect musculature beneath, and Erica felt her throat go dry. Why did he always affect her like this? she asked herself, sitting down to the breakfast she had just cooked for them both.

'We'll have to engage a housekeeper,' Rafe remarked, after she had popped back into the kitchen, returning with the butter-dish she had forgotten. 'I'm quite sure you won't want to do this every weekend.'

'Why not?' she quizzed, looking up, and saw from the familiar cynicism behind the cool mask of his features that he obviously thought the job beneath her. 'Why? Because you think housekeeping's too menial for me?' she pressed, hurt. Why would he never give her the benefit of the doubt? Start to see for himself that she wasn't the pretentious little snob he'd managed to convince himself she was?

Hard chips of sapphire rested on her where she sat, with her back to the window, where the sunlight streaming in lent a gold transparency to her hair. With disconcerting purpose those eyes roved across her face, tracing the fine brows above the wide brown eyes, the proud, straight nose and soft moue of her lips, moving with deliberate ease down the smooth column of her throat to the deep valley of her breasts just visible above the alluring satin, tinging her cheeks with soft colour. But whatever he was thinking, as his gaze lifted again, he said only, 'I don't want you tiring yourself out. You've got a demanding job, and I know for a fact I wouldn't find it much fun having to do a hard day's work and then come home and take on all the household chores as well.' She remembered him saying before they were married that he had someone who came in on a part-time basis during the week to clean, but the woman had left less than a week ago to emigrate with her son. 'Besides, I don't see why your office colleagues should have the best of you,' he stated drily, as he began opening the morning's post. 'When I come home at night, I'd at least like something of you for myself.'

So that was it! He wasn't just being kind, she realised, broodily watching the movement of those long, tapered fingers dealing with the mail. He just had to kill that snippet of consideration for her with a whip-cracking, chauvinistic remark like that!

He didn't see the hurt rebellion in her eyes, totally absorbed by the letter he had just opened, and a cursory glance at the envelope by his plate had Erica saying rather waspishly, 'Fan mail?' The Greek stamp hadn't escaped her notice, the beautiful, flowing writing clearly that of a woman.

'It's from Vikki. She's got a job over here,' Rafe offered succinctly, ignoring her tetchy comment, and folded the letter away in his pocket without another word.

'How nice for you!' Erica snapped, getting up, the other woman's frequent, irritating presence during their honeymoon too vivid in her mind. She had hung around constantly under the pretext of bringing groceries, or offering to show them the lesser known attractions of the island, so that once Rafe had even felt obliged to accept her hospitality. If obligation had come into it! Erica thought, peeved, collecting up the dishes with more than the necessary amount of clatter. After all, he hadn't seemed exactly averse to the other girl's very obvious designs on him, had he? she reminded herself with a festering poignancy as she reached for his empty plate. Then she started as hard fingers suddenly tightened around her wrist.

'Why don't you ask Myrtle if she'd like the job?' he said phlegmatically, his expression so disturbingly speculative, it took her a few moments to shrug off her uneasy thoughts and realise he'd reverted to their previous conversation.

'You mean...to come and live here?' A faint bloom of colour touched her cheeks. Was he really being considerate after all? He knew from the past how close she was to Myrtle, and the woman had commented at the wedding that she was often lonely in the dales between Sir Joshua's or Erica's visits, and Rafe had heard that.

'I would have though she was the natural choice.' His wry smile was heart-stopping, the pressure of his thumb as it stroked the blue, throbbing vein in her wrist sending a *frisson* of electrical pleasure through her. 'Just as long, of course, as your father doesn't mind her being poached.'

He wouldn't, and anyway, they could 'lend' her back to him whenever he went up to the cottage, Erica planned silently, her pulse resuming its normal pace again as Rafe released her. Myrtle would be thrilled, she thought, privately grateful to Rafe for suggesting it as she carried on stacking up the dishes, and she stole a sideways glance at him as he pushed back his chair and got up. The dark, casual clothes emphasised his rugged strength, though that innate elegance still shone through in the easy grace and economy of his movements—in the very authoritativeness of his presence—and being this close to him, while so lightly clothed herself, Erica felt her skin grow clammy, so that it was in a small, tremulous voice that she asked, 'Are you going to the sports centre now?' He had told her last night that today he'd be taking a casual look round a new sports complex for the disabled that his company had an interest in, and when he nodded, she said tentatively, 'Could...could I come with you?'

She surprised him as much as she surprised herself, she realised, when she saw the speculative puzzlement that darkened his eyes. Her request, though, wasn't only motivated by a need to win his favour, but by a genuine concern for those less fortunate than herself, and she was pleased when that dark head tilted in the briefest gesture of approval. 'Can you be ready in fifteen minutes?'

It was a tight schedule, but she was determined to adhere to it even if it killed her, and, seeing the mocking scepticism on that hard mouth, she said huskily, in answering challenge, 'Time me.'

Situated in a semi-rural part of town, the sports complex was a square, red-brick building enjoying an aspect of trees and open parkland and designed especially to cater for the leisure needs of the disabled. Fascinated, Erica watched young men and woman playing ball games from wheelchairs, saw children who were immobile for most of the time swimming in the clear, blue pool with more ease and confidence than she herself ever had, and outside, where a separate building housed a new riding stable, physically handicapped youngsters were discovering the joy of sitting on a horse for the very first time.

'It gives these children the confidence and independence they need,' one of the tutors told Erica as she was watching a small group of horses and young riders moving in a perfect figure of eight around the field. 'We thought at first we'd have to scrap horse-riding from our schedule because of the immense additional cost such a venture like this calls for, and it wouldn't have been possible out of council funds, but Cam-irrigation let us have this adjoining land for a song. These little riders have got a lot to thank your husband for, although their only concern when they arrive here is whether or not they each wind up with their favourite horse!'

Erica laughed at the woman's dry comment, looking over her shoulder for Rafe. He was on the other side of the field, talking to the centre's manager—his tall, commanding figure arresting even from this distance—and the knowledge that these children were able to enjoy themselves today because of his generosity touched her more than she could have realised.

How could so ruthless a man as he'd shown himself to be with her be so equally altruistic in other ways? she wondered emotionally, trying to understand the complexities of his nature, feeling that age-old admiration for him stir within her.

She was helping some teenage volunteers assist the children to dismount when he eventually joined her.

'I thought I'd still find you around the animals,' he drawled, cool mockery giving a lazy curve to his mouth. 'Been enjoying yourself?'

She nodded, fair hair moving gently, her face healthily glowing from the fresh March wind. 'The instructor said Cam-irrigation practically donated this land. I didn't realise you were such a philanthropist,' she commented, trying to keep her voice level—her respect for him well concealed—as she helped a small girl down from a gentle bay pony, delivering her safely into her father's waiting arms.

'No... well, we're all full of surprises, aren't we?' he expressed drily, when the man and the little girl were out of earshot, and one of the young assistants was leading the pony away. 'I wouldn't have thought helping disabled kids was exactly your idea of a Saturday morning's fun.'

She looked at him obliquely, tension knitting her fine brows. 'No?' Did he think her too superior even for that? 'No, well sometimes I come down off my pedestal just to please the ordinary people,' she returned corrosively—hurt—following his example and returning the instructor's friendly wave as she started walking with Rafe back to the car. 'You'd be surprised how pleasant these menials can be at times!'

Beside her, those powerful lungs inhaled sharply. 'All right—perhaps I deserved that.' He held open the gate for her leading on to the tarmacked area where they had left the car, shoulders broad and powerful beneath the chunky black sweater he wore over his shirt. 'What I was trying to say was I didn't realise you got on so well with children. I only hope you get as much enjoyment from our own kids when they arrive.'

Guilty, lashes lowered, she couldn't look at him as they reached the BMW. How could he know how much that simple statement could hurt?

'One of those men in that pool today was a thalidomide victim,' she digressed sympathetically, needing a diversion, quietly reflective for a moment as she got into the car. What cruel agony those unfortunate mothers must have suffered, she thought shiveringly, after months of probable anticipated joy! 'That's one case that bears out the fact of animal experiments not being reliable,' she went on with a determined thrust to her chin as Rafe settled in beside her. 'Another's penicillin. In contrast, it works wonders for the human race, but if the effects on some animals had been taken into account earlier the drug would never have been marketed. There are a whole host of others, too, that have been tested safe with animals and then been used on humans with drastic side effects—even fatal results! Apart from the moral issue, animal experimentation wastes time and money because when a drug's proved safe through the use of some poor defenceless creature research has to be done all over again to establish its effect on humans.' She shrugged as she fastened her seatbelt, aware of Rafe doing the same. 'It's been a long, slow process, but in our labs we've managed to begin to phase out a considerable amount of the animal research we do, but some of the pharmacologists still want to hang on to the old methods—refuse to accept real science methods as a better alternative. They're still of the opinion that abusing animals is the only way to save human lives.'

'And by real science methods you mean . . . cell and tissue culture . . . analytical techniques . . . things like that.' Her surprise must have shown, because that firm mouth pulled down one side and he said softly, 'My father was a scientist, too, remember?' He started the engine, but didn't pull away, angling towards her with his arm across the back of her seat instead. 'So tell me more,' he invited.

'Do you really want to know?' Heat stole across her skin from his nearness, his sudden, undivided attention.

He nodded, black hair shining like jet as it caught the sun.

'Well,' she proceeded, cheeks flushed with enthusiasm for a subject close to her heart and which she had studied well, not only from books but from long, interesting hours in the laboratory. 'It's possible to keep cells from almost any human organ alive for . . . practically as long as you like nowadays. Tissue can be grown exactly representing the tissue of the human body, and through it viruses, genetic defects and other things like hormones can be studied. Also, with the added aid of computers—instead of animals,' she interjected emphatically with a grimace, 'our pharmacologists can study the actions of a new drug on any human organ, cutting out the need for animal experimentation completely. The end result is more reliable and humane research and drugs that don't produce results like...well...' She shrugged. 'Thalidomide.' She went on, informing him of further methods of research that were being used now in schools and universities which eliminated vivisection while he listened without interruption, silently interested.

That, she remembered, was something else she had always loved and admired about him—his ability to listen—and now she saw a smile touch his lips, an eyebrow lifting slightly. 'You've become a real authority on the subject, haven't you?' he commented. 'I was always surprised though that you chose to go into the business in the first place, knowing how sensitively you feel about animals. Because, as you said yourself, they still play a major role in drug research—even under your father's own flag.'

'So I should run away and pretend it doesn't exist?' She sent him a half-deprecating smile. 'Anyway, Dad has very stringent rules about the humanity of tests carried out in the labs, even though I, personally, consider them all to be morally wrong. Besides,' she met his gaze levelly with a toss of pale hair, resolve in every neat angle of her fine features, 'if you're fighting a war— doing your darnedest to change other people's opinions—you don't do it from the other side of the world.'

Silently, his gaze tugged over her, something flickering in those blue depths. A glimmer of...what? Ap-

proval? she wondered, achingly wanting his respect—
the affection he'd once shown her—above everything
else.

'No,' he breathed then, and with such vehemence—
such hardening of that strong face as he rammed the car
into gear that she wondered what private battle he might
be fighting himself for him to have reacted like that.

Really, she knew so little about the real man behind
that hard veneer, she thought, as he drove them back to
town, in spite of their heady, passionate involvement five
years ago. But she had been little more than a child then,
her own character barely developed, and she had been
too wrapped up in her own consuming emotions to notice
too deeply how he felt himself—what made him tick.
Certainly, she had had no inkling of the bitter-sweet
brutality he would be capable of employing in his long-
suffering need to punish her, that utter demoralising of
her through her own sensuality in a continual bending
of her will to his which, over the weeks, made her tense
and reticent, determined to conceal any emotion from
him. It was difficult, though, restraining her laughter in
situations they often found mutually amusing, or her
enthusiasm when his appreciation of literature, art and
music corresponded so completely with her own. But
she felt as if the effort was wearing her out because she
was often tired these days, falling asleep at the drop of
a hat, which wasn't like her. She was working hard in
the office, but, with Myrtle having happily agreed to her
request and keeping house for her and Rafe now, it
shouldn't have bothered her too much, and she could
only deduce that both the strain of her marriage and her
worries over her father were taking their toll. That was
until she decided she might be deficient in some vitamin
and went to the doctor, only to receive the biggest shock
of her life.

CHAPTER FIVE

PREGNANT? Expecting a *baby*? But how could she be? she wondered, numb with shock and disbelief, leaving the doctor's surgery that day in an electrified daze. How could it have happened to her, she asked incredulously—bewildered—when all along she'd been told how unlikely it was, when she had taken no precautions, so certain that she'd be safe? Her cycle had been so irregular, she'd had no indication she'd conceived, but the result of the test was definitely positive, and now, as her thinking processes began to return, unhappily she wondered what would have happened if she had married Rafe when he'd first asked her to five years ago. Would she have conceived so easily? At all? Had all the heart-searching pain, the misery and the broken dreams been for nothing? Could they have had a happy, normal relationship, after all?

Agony tore at her as she steeled herself not to think about the past, the reality of the present descending on her like a stifling black fog. This wasn't five years ago, this was here and now, and suddenly all she could feel was frighteningly trapped—trapped in a loveless marriage with a man who now virtually hated her, she reminded herself with tortured acceptance—wanting to cry, to laugh, to scream out against the bitter irony of it all.

'He didn't waste much time, did he?' was the blunt comment from Myrtle when Erica came home and told her that evening, although she could see from the way the elderly face glowed that the other woman was quietly delighted. 'I hadn't realised he was so much of a family man—that he'd want you starting a baby straight away.'

Helping Myrtle chop some vegetables in the large, modern kitchen, Erica tensed, not telling the house-keeper that to make her pregnant had been one of Rafe's main aims in this marriage, and probably only because he realised his power in the company would be doubly strengthened with an heir. Neither had she ever told Myrtle of the doctors' pessimistic outlook for her chances of motherhood all those years ago, her inadequacy, something she hadn't liked talking about with anyone, something she'd always almost been ashamed of. And now...

'You'll have to take things easier, my girl, and not overtax yourself dashing about that office.' Myrtle was enjoying making a fuss—not noticing how subdued she was—Erica realised through a tumult of emotions, re-lieved, because she couldn't begin to explain to the other woman how she was feeling right then. But tension knotted the muscles at the nape of her neck at Myrtle's sudden querying, 'Have you told Rafe?'

'Yes...he was pleased,' Erica answered truthfully, since he'd known where she had been going that morning and had insisted on meeting her afterwards. But, stirring the delicious-smelling contents of a pot that was sim-mering on the stove, she refrained from telling the older woman about the scene that had ensued between them.

'Well, you've got what you want,' she'd told Rafe pointedly when they were seated in the little restaurant where he had taken her for lunch. 'Now you've got to give me what I want...and also——' She'd broken off, the daunting lift of a black eyebrow making her swallow nervously. 'From now on, Rafe, I want separate bedrooms.'

'Do you?' The firm mouth had twitched half humor-ously, the spark that had lit his eyes when she'd told him about the baby suddenly extinguished as they glittered like blue ice. 'No,' he'd replied peremptorily then, his voice deep and low across the intimate table, adding in firm conclusion, 'On both counts.'

Dumbfounded, she'd stared at him slicing calmly through his steak in angry disbelief, her hair falling over her shoulder like a slick trail of honey, while her knife had clattered noisily against the plate of crab salad she'd barely touched.

And he'd said simply, 'While you're carrying my child, Erica, you'll share my bed as well.' He'd glanced up, those blue eyes intent, probing the mutinous depths of hers. 'And things can...happen...during the early stages of pregnancy, I believe,' he stated with a hard, cynical emphasis, 'so where that evidence is concerned, darling, you'll just have to be patient a little longer.'

'Why?' She hadn't been able to help flinging back at him. 'Just in case I consider getting rid of it?' That was what he had meant, of course, and she had had to stifle a small, choked sob, not wanting him to know how much it had hurt her to say it.

Of course, she would never have considered abortion. New life was growing inside of her—something she had never quite dared to hope for. *Her* baby. Rafe's baby. Deep down inside she'd felt a warmth begin to flood through her, and could never have admitted to him, to anyone, hardly even to herself then that, despite her fears and forebodings, she was realising a long-lost, secret ambition. Rafe's child! Crazily, one moment she'd felt like shouting it out at the top of her voice, so bursting with emotion she'd wanted the restaurant—the whole world!—to know what impossible little miracle had happened to her that day; the next, cursing fate for allowing it to happen at all—now—when she didn't have his love, when all chance of her happiness with him had, indirectly, been robbed by that brutal prognosis five years ago.

'Come along.' His eyes had been hooded and dark, his voice so gentle as he'd led her out of the restaurant that she'd wondered if he'd guessed at the turmoil going on inside her. But, of course, he couldn't have, she thought now—reminding herself of how much he thought she despised him—though he'd insisted on walking her back to the office, surprising her when he'd stopped to buy a single white rose from a flower-seller in the busy market, causing her heart to leap ridiculously when he had drawn the delicate, moist bloom lightly across her cheek, and, inclining his dark head, had murmured against her lips, 'That's for being a very clever girl.' It might have been a genuine compliment from a proud father-to-be to his very adored wife, she reflected, remembering that strange inflexion in his voice, the darkening emotion in those beautiful eyes, but now she turned away from Myrtle's shrewd pair with tears in hers, telling herself that her condition was just making her fanciful—over-emotional—because she knew better than that.

Over the weeks that followed, life continued reasonably smoothly. Surprisingly, Erica found she had few ill-effects from her pregnancy, continuing with her job, although things were different now that Rafe was around the office. He was, she realised enviously, one of those people who seemed to get forty-eight hours out of every day, finding time, in spite of his other commitments, to put his reorganisation plans for Witneys into operation. From that first morning he strode on to the company's premises the impact of his presence was staggering, that motivating male energy and authority making itself felt almost immediately from senior management level right down to the office junior.

'No wonder he's such a success story!' Unintentionally concealed behind the shelves of files in the new records office one afternoon, Erica couldn't help overhearing as two young female clerks came in. 'He doesn't stand for any messing about or inefficiency, yet he still manages to make you like working for him.'

'Surprise, surprise!' the other voice laughed. 'It's because he's so darn sexy and good-looking. I wouldn't mind being told what to do by a man like that any day of the week!'

'No. Lucky Erica. I'll bet he's a stupendous lover! It was a hell of a shock to me though when he suddenly married her like that,' the first girl expressed, making Erica stiffen, listen with a sudden, acute interest now. 'My brother works at Cam-irrigation, and, according to people there, rumour had it that wedding bells were ringing for him with someone he was heavily involved with in Greece.'

With Vikki Stavros? Pain, swift and killing, shot across Erica's heart. It couldn't be anyone else. Had he really loved Vikki, then, but let his business interests rule his emotions when he had decided to marry *her*? she wondered achingly as the two girls went out, leaving her silent presence unrevealed. Stupidly, she'd half hoped that there was more behind his marrying her than just the sealing of a comfortable business arrangement—that deep inside he still retained some of the affection he had shown her as a doting adolescent. But had he loved Vikki all along? Was that why she was coming over here as he'd related to Erica so casually that day they'd gone to the sports centre—because he was still in love with the beautiful Greek girl?

The thought was too unbearable to entertain as she found the file she'd been looking for and hurried back to her office, although reluctantly she had to accept that one thing the young clerk had said was true. Rafe *was* motivating. Witneys seemed to buzz with a new electrical energy these days, even if she did resent his being there, because his active involvement—however unwelcome where she was concerned—was producing the new streamlined effect the company needed.

Surprisingly, too, when they were in the office he treated her as a respected equal, inviting her opinions and ideas with far more enthusiasm than her other male colleagues or even her father ever had, so that working with Rafe became unexpectedly exciting and stimulating, stretching her mind to capacity—their avid discussions and exchanges of views which nowadays slid beyond work to their social hours an exhilarating pleasure for her that she knew the girl she had been five years ago would have been far too young even to comprehend.

Dear heaven! Why did she love him this much? It was a small, desperate prayer, uttered through her agonised, hopeless longing for him, one day when he was away— tied up in his own business affairs abroad—because she couldn't deny it any longer. She didn't think she had ever really stopped loving him. Her feelings had been merely frozen—locked in ice when she'd let herself believe he was Laverne's lover, his denial setting in a thaw she hadn't wanted or welcomed so that, now he was away, life seemed dull and empty without him, and she was missing him terribly. Consequently, it was difficult hiding her pleasure from him when he returned towards the end of May, looking lithe, fit and superbly tanned. Only she knew just how hard her heart thudded when she saw him step through the door of the apartment— how her breath caught from the impact of his sheer, physical presence—so that she had no defence against that raw sexuality as he pulled her hard into his arms, having needed him too long not to welcome those lips burning fever across her skin, inviting the touch of his hands on her body with an excitement that annihilated all pride and self-respect, ignoring the little voices of her degradation for the inevitable and explosive pleasure that lay in surrender.

'I'm arranging to have a few people round on Saturday night,' he told her the following evening over dinner, topping up her glass with mineral water. 'I know you were thinking of seeing some friends from the office for a meal that evening, but I'd like you to be here if you could.'

She nodded in acquiescence, eyes drawn to the dark, sinewy strength of his hand filling his own glass with red wine. 'What are we celebrating?' she queried, interested, hair stirring with a gentle movement of her head.

'I want to show your father's colleagues that there is a human side to this ogre that's been forced upon them,' Rafe went on to explain, a smile tugging at the firm mouth. 'The hours I spend at Witneys don't allow for any socialising and I think it would benefit us all to see each other away from the office for a change—meet in more relaxed surroundings.'

'So you just throw a party to win them all over—just as you've managed to do with Dad?' Finishing her lasagne, Erica put down her knife and fork with a resounding little clatter, her eyes dark pools of accusation. She knew she was being unnecessarily irritable, but she couldn't help it, the reminder that he had got exactly what he wanted out of this marriage—a dictating say in Witneys—when he still wasn't fulfilling his part of the bargain a very sore point with her today. He was still putting off helping Sir Joshua with that evidence, and, though she'd virtually begged him to again only last night, he'd refused.

'No,' he said then, getting up and going across to put a disc into the hi-fi. 'Whether I've got them on my side or not doesn't particularly worry me. I've got a job to do and I intend to see that it's done properly and effectively, and if I happen to put a few noses out of joint in the process—well, that's too bad. Your father put his company into my hands because he considered me the best man for the job—whether you or anyone else like it or not—but he is still the head of the firm and as such I would have hoped his strength and judgement could have been shown more respect—at least by his own daughter.' His tone admonished, lips compressing, and a muscle pulled in the strong jaw. 'Still, I've never flattered myself I'd get the same unconditional co-operation from you in helping me carry out his wishes as I seem to have been honoured with from you in bed.'

Colour tinged her cheeks, and as Elgar's music filled the large room she got up, knocking the table clumsily.

'Do you really think I *like* making love with you?' she exhaled, trying to inject a degree of self-disgust into her voice as she saw him getting up off his haunches. 'You might have other women ready to fall into bed with you, but, quite honestly, if I didn't have to endure it I wouldn't.' And as she crossed to the door, 'Really, it just makes me sick!'

She didn't realise how quickly he could move until she felt the tenacious grip of his fingers bite into her wrist, pull her round to face the naked anger in his eyes.

'Well, well.' There was a cynical curve to his lips now, a softly threatening quality to his voice that sent a little shiver down her spine. 'And I really thought you were getting as much pleasure out of it as I was. Which just goes to show how we must never assume anything, must we?'

'No, Rafe!'

He was dragging her towards the settee, and she let
out a sharp cry as he pulled her down after him across
his lap, the soft leather giving beneath their weight.

'So I've been imagining those little murmurs of
pleasure, have I?' he taunted, his lips suddenly burning
a heart-thumping trail across her cheek. 'And I've mis-
calculated your body's responsiveness to me when I touch
you, obviously,' he breathed, one hand lifting with a
blatant insolence to the soft, warm curve of her breast
through her silky blouse.

She drew in her breath, her senses swimming—assailed by his hard, masculine strength. He smelt fresh
and clean, his hair still slightly damp from the shower
he had taken when he had come in, his rousing warmth
burning into her. 'So I was imagining it all, was I?' he
goaded softly, feeling, as tangibly as she did, the betraying hardening of her nipple beneath the tormenting
action of his thumb.

Shamed by her involuntary response to him, mutinously she turned her face from the hard satisfaction she
saw in his, but he laughed softly, and shifted his position, the arm behind her head forcing her closer, so
that there was no way she escape the crushing domi-
nation of his mouth.

She pushed against him hard, but his arms were relentless. His kiss, though, had become less demanding,
almost unbearably tender, his tongue probing the inner
recesses of her mouth.

His scent, his warmth, the feel of his hands, were like
necessary drugs to her, and instinctively she pressed
herself against him, her breathing quickening as every
starved sense fed on the throbbing relief it sought. She
felt him tremble, his embrace tighten painfully, and she
made a sound like a soft purr, her arm curling around
his neck, all pride swamped by the aching need inside

her, by the arousing power of his body, and the hard, fulfilling pleasure it promised.

Then he lifted his head, and she uttered a choking sob, hers falling back in a cascade of blonde silk.

He was gazing down at her, his lashes black and thick against the wells of his eyes. He looked flushed, she thought hazily—oddly vulnerable—her own desire reflected in her heavy, slumbrous eyes, in the warm colour spreading upwards across her cheekbones, in the firm, betraying peaks of her breasts. And through her languid senses she heard him say softly, mockingly, 'Going to be sick, Erica?'

His words stung like silken whips and, hurt, shamed by her own weakness, she tugged out of his grasp, stumbling away from the settee.

'I'm sorry, darling, but you should know better than to make such profoundly inaccurate statements,' he expressed, getting up, his apology purely superficial. 'We both know that in one aspect of this marriage you're as completely obsessed as I am. And don't try to deny it, dearest, because you make a very poor liar. You want me, and no matter what sick excuse you might try and make about the reason for it you know as well as I do that I only have to touch you and every single high-falutin principle you have just crumbles to dust.'

She turned her head sharply away as he moved closer to her, feeling her secrets stripped with a rawness that equalled the ache in the pit of her stomach, because she knew he was right.

'So what?' she returned with an attempt at nonchalance, staring through the window at the panorama of the city so that he wouldn't see the wounded pride mirrored in her eyes. 'It's only sex.'

She heard him laugh softly just behind her. 'I was under the impression that for a woman there had to be something more—a subconscious selecting of the most suitable candidate to father her offspring, rather than giving into those instinctive needs for needs' sake.'

He was right, of course. Nevertheless, she turned round to say pointedly, 'Like a man, you mean?' He didn't answer, and she glanced back at the window, saying with a sudden weariness, 'That's a Victorian myth.' Her gaze followed the progress of a car along the road, way below, on the other side of the river, the late May sunset striking fire across its tinted windows. 'That's just something man dreamed up for fear his woman might start behaving with the same freedom he's always allowed himself—or to boost his ego as to why any woman wants to go to bed with him!' She didn't believe what she was saying, but she went on, 'So you see, you've been rather misguided, Rafe,' and, turning to look at him, she added with a careless little shrug, 'We're really quite as cold-blooded beneath those age-old theories as you men are.' She had to keep him believing that, otherwise she knew she would never be able to survive the humiliation of his realising the truth: that he was the only man who had ever made her blood sing, made her sob with desire; that she was in love with him—even though all he wanted was to make her pay for her supposed wrongs in the past—and that in the process she had less self-respect than the loveless, pleasure-seeking little wanton she wanted to convince him she was.

Something glimmered in those blue eyes, and he started to say something. But Myrtle came in at that moment to clear the dinner table, and, gratefully, Erica took advantage of the other woman's presence to get away.

CHAPTER SIX

THE social gathering Rafe had arranged that weekend held more surprises than Erica had bargained for, particularly when Graham Caddis turned up as one of the guests.

'Why did you have to invite *him*?' she snapped at Rafe when Myrtle showed the younger man in with Sir Joshua Witney. Across the heads of several earlier arrivals, she returned her father's warm smile, aware of Rafe's close scrutiny shifting from her face to the flattering cream dolman-sleeved dress she wore.

'Perhaps I just wanted to see your reaction, darling,' he answered, the smile he gave her emblazoned with such charm that only she wasn't fooled into thinking her husband was in love with her as he moved away with that inherent grace of his to receive his latest guests.

'You're looking well, Erica.' Graham's cool comment was purely conversational, she realised, when good manners forced her into following Rafe's example to greet him at the door. But she wanted to speak with her father and, unobtrusively, she reached up to kiss his gaunt cheek.

'Are you taking care of yourself,' she whispered, her heart aching from the knowledge that Rafe could be so cold-blooded to put off clearing his name when the charges hanging over her father were clearly not helping his health. He looked so drawn and pale.

'Stop worrying about me, dear.' A paternal hand patted hers and a smile brightened watery blue eyes as he studied his daughter approvingly. 'At least *you* seem to be doing something right. You look positively blooming.'

'Yes, she does, doesn't she?' Graham, overhearing, reinforced, and, with a grudging glance in Rafe's direction, added with unveiled resentment, 'Marriage seems to be agreeing with her.'

She didn't tell either of them that it was probably because she was pregnant, that her outward appearance didn't reflect her mental state at all. But her pregnancy was something she wanted to keep within the four walls of her home until the changing shape of her body spoke for itself. At present she didn't think she could bear the happy surprise and congratulations which would follow such a revelation when she was so unhappy herself, when the father of her child despised her—and would always despise her for the things he had believed about her, still believed about her now.

'Pity you missed your chance, Caddis.' Wry cynicism was woven into Rafe's deep, Scots drawl, and his arm came to rest proprietorially across Erica's shoulders. 'To protect your interests in this life, lad, you have to grab your opportunities at every turn of the road.'

'Well you certainly did that, didn't you?' Graham's feigned amusement didn't reach his eyes and his voice dropped, his tone suddenly becoming more personal as Sir Joshua was drawn away by another guest. 'You've got the girl and a nice hand in Witneys with one effortless stroke. Nice move, Cameron. I envy your style.' There was a sort of cruel malice in the smile Graham gave her, and Erica felt slightly sick, sensing that he'd come pretty close to guessing just why Rafe had married her.

She hardly heard his slick reply, alive only to the arm tightening about her in a gesture that was wholly possessive, bringing her into startling contact with the hard angles of his body. 'I just hope your business acumen

is more reliable than your luck with women, Caddis,'
the deep tones drawled then. 'Witneys needs tightening
up and I was hoping to do it without any casualties.'

Suddenly he was the employer—dogmatic, omnip-
otent and hard—and she saw Graham's face blanch
before he shot her one swift, killing look, then rapidly
made himself scarce.

'Just who do you think you are?' Angrily, Erica pulled
away from Rafe, her face flooding with hot colour. 'You
haven't any right to threaten my father's staff like that!'
She didn't like the way Graham was behaving towards
her, but she couldn't stand by and see him being treated
unfairly. 'Graham is a very respected member of the firm,
and I'll have you know his sales record is second to
none!'

Hard lines deepened around the firm, masculine
mouth and jaw. 'Then he doesn't have anything to worry
about, does he, darling?' he assured her with a cool
smile, that hard, masculine composure conveying just
how much controlling power he had in the company—
and that he would use it if he had to.

She was surprised, though, as the party got under way,
to realise how respected and liked he seemed to have
become in so short a time. Men older than he was weren't
too proud to ask his advice, while younger members of
the staff, eager to speak to him, hovered constantly in
his sphere, young male faces glowing with satisfaction
when eventually they got their chance, the females among
them unable to hide their appreciation of Rafe's dark
good looks and charm, their voices, Erica couldn't help
overhearing, high-pitched and a little tense, every
movement and mannerism designed to gain the attention of a very attractive man.

She had gone into the kitchen to help Myrtle with the
food, and paused in the lounge doorway, a plate in each
hand, surprised by the number of people who filled the

room now. Most of them worked at Witneys, although she knew Rafe had also invited one or two of his more social acquaintances along for the evening. She could see him now, standing a good head above everyone else, talking to someone on the other side of the room, hair sleek and black, authority stamped on every line of that hard, well-sculpted face, a sheer, male magnetism that even as Erica watched had female eyes turning his way, had desire coiling painfully in her own stomach.

'Can't take your eyes off him, can you?' She started, nearly dropping one of the plates, her surprise at seeing Vikki Stavros utterly total. 'There *are* other people in the room!'

Was there sarcasm in that soft, accented voice? Erica wondered, wishing she hadn't been so mesmerised by Rafe's obvious attraction just when Vikki had to appear! She looked lovely, too, in a snug-fitting, wrap-around red dress, her black hair, swept provocatively back one side and secured with a silver slide, enhancing the glowing, Mediterranean complexion, the full, creamy red lips.

'I didn't realise you were coming.' With a calmness she was suddenly far from feeling, Erica walked over to the buffet table and put the plates down. 'Rafe didn't mention it,' she said, meeting the other woman's dark eyes levelly, her own, gold hair, coiled into a smooth knot, giving an added elegance to the proud column of her throat.

'That sounds like Rafe.' Vikki laughed, sending a sultry glance in his direction. 'When you get to know him as long as I have you'll discover that he often forgets *unimportant* things.' From the emphasis with which she conveyed it, Erica gathered that the Greek girl considered herself anything but, biting back a childish urge to remind Vikki that *she'd* known Rafe far longer. 'I suppose he's mentioned that I'm living here now?' And without waiting for a reply, 'I'm sorry if I embarrassed you when I caught you secretly devouring him just now.' She was apologising almost as if she meant it. 'But then he's the most delicious-looking animal, isn't he? Can we help ourselves?'

'Certainly...to the food, Vikki,' Erica responded meaningfully as tanned, red-tipped fingers daintily selected a prawn vol-au-vent from the table.

'What else?' Vikki gave a little laugh, sinking white teeth into the soft pastry case, though the thin line between the ebony eyebrows told Erica her warning had registered. 'Did you make these yourself?' Erica nodded—not elaborating that she had spent half the afternoon enjoying herself helping Myrtle prepare all the little savouries and desserts—and she saw the fine brows lift. 'I somehow never imagined Rafe marrying someone...domestic!'

It could have been a compliment but Erica had the distinct impression that it had been meant in a detrimental sense. Or was she imagining things, just letting her prejudices rule her? she wondered uneasily.

Ten minutes later, when she was talking to another couple, she was certain she wasn't when she glanced up and saw Vikki across the room, sharing some lighthearted joke with Rafe. She could hear her stimulated laughter over the hum of party conversation, her eyes, as she looked up at him, adoring and dark. Then someone shouldered past and she saw Rafe draw Vikki out of the other man's way, the arm that lay briefly across her shoulders inducing hers to slip brazenly around his waist.

Heavens! She was so obvious! Erica thought resentfully. But was it all totally unprovoked? What were Rafe's feelings for the other girl? And did Vikki know why he had married her? Had he told her that she was expecting his baby? she wondered with a harrowing anguish—tortured from not knowing—turning away from the sight of those red nails against her husband's dark jacket to move among her other guests, smiling out her role as hostess until her jaw ached.

Alone, beside the balcony windows—open on to the night—she overheard Graham, a little distance away, agreeing almost too eagerly with something her father was saying, and through her silent wretchedness she cringed. He was very much a yes-man, she thought, though she had never realised it when they had been going out together, feeling a little peeved at having to admit that Rafe had assessed his character correctly from the beginning, while she hadn't been able to see it until now.

'I never thought I'd find myself envying a lump of feelingless crystal.' Rafe was at her side, gaze resting on the soft curve of her lips, and, discomfited by the desire she recognised in him, she looked down at the clear, sparkling mineral water in her glass, taking a deep, antagonised breath.

'Been deserted, Rafe?' She glanced up again, hiding her innermost emotions behind an almost nonchalant air, suddenly very conscious of the other woman's absence from the party.

'If you mean has Vikki left, the answer's yes,' he stated, and she wondered why he sounded so impatient suddenly. Was he missing the other girl already? she thought with a tearing pain deep down inside. 'She had another appointment, and would have said goodbye to you but you were tied up with someone else,' he informed her, slipping a hand into the pocket of his trousers, their snug fit emphasising the narrow angles of his hips, the long, powerful legs. 'She was sorry she couldn't stay.'

I'll bet she was! Erica had to bite down hard to stop herself saying it. Please heaven let him think she didn't care! Instead, she sent an unwitting glance towards the gaunt, white-haired figure of her father, still talking to Graham, and she noticed how Rafe's mouth hardened.

'He isn't very well,' she said woundedly, worried about Sir Joshua. 'And it's all your fault. You could have a little more feeling!' This was in a heated whisper as people were glancing their way, assessing, no doubt, their differing qualities, because she knew they made a striking couple, her blonde petiteness comparable with Rafe's dark strength, the grace and elegance with which he carried himself a complement, had she but realised it, to her own chic femininity.

'Just as you did when it amused you to play around with me.' His deep voice condemned. 'Having your fun and then distorting the facts to suit yourself before running off to Switzerland without a thought for anyone but Erica Witney?' He moved in close, one hand on the wall behind her, making her so aware of him that her breath seemed to scorch her lungs. She was held captive by more than just that evidence—and he knew it! she realised hopelessly, the softly golden hair almost touching that forceful jaw as she lifted her head.

'I didn't ...' she began in defence of herself. Then, tremulously, 'Anyway, that's different. I was only seventeen, so I think I can be forgiven for jumping to the conclusion I did.'

'Oh? So you finally believe me, do you?' His eyes were inky black, penetrating hers with a sabre-like quality that seemed to reach down to her soul, turning her bones to liquid. Yes, she believed him now, knew that deep down inside part of her had always wanted to believe him, that he had been right when he'd accused her of using what she'd seen as an excuse to get away, subconsciously unable to cope with the thought of his rejection of her if she'd told him the truth. He might be unscrupulous, but not to the point of involving himself with another man's wife; in womanhood she could accept that without any doubt now, and she glanced away from those probing chips of sapphire to utter, 'Anyone can make a mistake. And you weren't exactly the optimum judge of character yourself, were you? No matter what you like to think, Rafe, I never once thought myself better than you—or anyone else. I never have.'

His eyes glittered with some dark emotion, veiled in an instant by those long black lashes. 'What is this, Erica—a purging of the soul?' His words were softly mocking, and she drew a sharp breath, realising her incautious admission. 'If that's the case, then why wouldn't you marry me?' he pressed, and suddenly there were only the two of them in the room, the past seeming to seal them in a small bubble of intimacy. 'Or was amusement really all it was to you, little cat?' Something tautened the structure of that handsome face—at variance with the soft control with which he spoke—and she had to restrain the urge to run her fingers down the proud line of his cheek, soothe away the tension that gripped him, for one rash moment wanting to tell him the truth. But if she did, he would guess how much he had meant to her—still meant to her, she realised achingly—and she didn't know if her pride could stand that. He didn't love her. She wasn't naïve enough to imagine that he did. And if he realised that she had deceived him—married him, thinking herself infertile—then he might easily take out his obvious anger by refusing to help Sir Joshua.

She looked at him obliquely. 'Is it really that important to you, Rafe?' Her voice was cool as she put the onus back on him, a mock confidence hiding her inner turmoil though her cheeks were burning from the heavy beating of her heart, making her glad of the cooling air from the balcony.

'You really know how to play this game, don't you?' Those heavy lids hid any emotion, but his voice was oddly raw against the buzz of conversation around them—the distant hum of traffic from the city below— and the masculine chest flexed as if he were holding something on a tight leash and only just succeeding. 'What do you want me to say, Erica? That it was hell living without you?' Her gaze—dark with hope—darted searchingly to his, but his mouth curved in a cynical smile, his face giving nothing away. 'Would it please that fickle, feminine heart of yours, dearest, to have me dangling like some puppet? Something you could cut down at the slightest whim?' She could feel his breath against her temple, warm and uneven as it seemed almost to be dragged through those strong, masculine lungs, his voice, his scent, his utter nearness acting on her like some erotic drug. 'Haven't you ever heard of the phrase "Once bitten..."?' He uttered a cruel, curt laugh. 'I'm sorry, darling. But I shan't be falling into that trap again.'

Grooves etched his face, making him look grim, yet strangely tired, and her eyes scanned the dark, inscrutable depths of his, heart fluttering from the startling realisation of just how much she had hurt him, suddenly aching for a glimmer of the love she had once had and lost.

Emotion clogged her throat as she started to speak, but then someone touched his arm, a portly, middle-aged man she knew vaguely from Quality Control who said jovially, 'Be a bit sporting, Cameron. You can have her twenty-four hours a day, so let some of us less fortunate chaps have her for a few minutes.' And with a mischievous little wink at Erica, 'Or is he likely to beat you if he finds you talking to another man?'

Her forced smile barely concealed her frustration at his untimely intrusion, although Rafe looked remarkably unaffected, once more the urbane, charming host.

'OK, Grierson,' he assented drily, lips compressing. 'But only for five minutes. After that I get the whip out, and you wouldn't want me to mar that beautiful soft skin, would you?'

He might have been joking, but, as he allowed her out of his disturbing sphere, impetuously Erica considered that she would rather have taken that sort of treatment from him than the bitter-sweet torture of loving him when he'd clearly closed his heart to her for good.

But later, when she was alone in bed, as Rafe was still discussing some business with a colleague in his study, a small ray of optimism shone through her bleak emotions, assuring her that nothing was impossible. If he had loved her once, then surely she could make him love her again? After all, they had something very much in common in the child they had both created. So when the baby was born, she reasoned hopefully, surely his joy at being a father would help to assuage this bitterness in him—this cold, ironlike barrier he had erected against her—make him respect and care for her again if only as the mother of his child? But if there was to be any hope of that, then she had to be very careful not to let him know the secret she had kept from him, otherwise he might guess at the revenge she had been planning when he had forced her into marrying him, and that could only make matters worse. But she *would* have his love again, she determined, feeling considerably happier as she finally drifted into sleep.

She woke to find the other half of the bed rumpled but empty, and hazily remembered Rafe telling her he had business in Norfolk that day.

Pulling on jeans and a very feminine white top, knotted at the waist, she spent a few hasty moments applying mascara and a pale pink lipstick after she had washed, keen to make herself look attractive, before brushing her long blonde hair until it shone.

Myrtle was in the kitchen preparing breakfast when Erica entered, but there was no sign of Rafe.

'He went out early,' the woman revealed at Erica's enquiry.

'But he wasn't supposed to be leaving until ten!' She glanced at the modern clock over the door showing twenty minutes to and flopped down at the kitchen table, nursing an idiotic disappointment. Now she'd have to wait until the following day before he returned. 'You should have woken me up before he went,' she groaned.

'He asked me not to—said that you needed your rest.' Erica smiled wanly at Myrtle's maternal-like firmness as the woman set cereal and a glass of orange juice down in front of her. 'You had a late night last night, my lass, and I can understand why he didn't want to disturb you. Besides, the phone rang just after eight and he didn't stop for any breakfast himself. I don't know what it was she wanted but it must have been important because he shot off like a bat out of hell.'

'She?' Erica surveyed her curiously, eyes narrowing. 'Do you know who it was?' she asked, heart missing a beat.

'Some lass with an accent. Vikki somebody, I think she said.' An elderly hand pushed back a strand of greying hair. 'Is that his secretary?' dazedly Erica heard Myrtle enquiring. 'Or someone to do with the conference he said was going to today?'

'What? Oh...probably,' she faltered, not wanting to lie, but not knowing what else to say, averting her gaze from the older woman because she knew the colour had drained out of her cheeks, that her expression was stunned and tortured from the sharp, knife-like pain that had seemed to rip across her heart.

So Vikki had telephoned and he had gone to her—just like that, she realised injuredly, without bothering to wake her to say 'goodbye', without even eating, driving off to meet the other woman even though he had an important conference to attend today.

Jealousy mingled with hurt anger tore at her insides, making her feel giddy, slightly sick. Oh, goodness! What stupid dreams had she been weaving last night when she had believed that she could make him love her? It was Vikki he cared about—it had to be—if he could go to her as soon as she rang him, putting her above everything else.

She didn't know how she got through the day. Hour after hour dragged. She tried to work on a new advertising concept from the file she'd brought home on Friday night, but no ideas would come, her mind tortured by thoughts of Rafe—the way he'd left to see Vikki that morning as if nothing else had mattered.

Eventually, needing to get out, she rang a friend from the office, suggesting that they meet for dinner, the result of which was an exotic Indian meal in a little restaurant in the West End, so that her low spirits had lifted a little by the time she returned home.

She woke feeling groggy and couldn't understand why. It hadn't been a particularly late night, and she had had nothing strong to drink, having wisely abstained from alcohol ever since she'd found out she was pregnant. Therefore she could only assume it was a rare bout of morning sickness, although by the time she reached the office she had a headache and a pain, too, deep in the pit of her stomach.

'You look frightful,' her secretary remarked as Erica stepped through the door. 'You aren't sickening for flu or anything, are you?'

Lightly, Erica shrugged off the other girl's suggestion. No one knew yet that she was expecting a baby as, amazingly, in spite of her former internal problems, she had had very few of the usual symptoms accompanied by early pregnancy. Even the doctor had informed her with pleasant surprise that she was the perfect example of a healthy mum-to-be.

Bravely, she took the onslaught of a particularly hectic morning until suddenly, around lunchtime, she had such a gripping spasm of pain in her lower body she had to clutch at the desk to stop herself from doubling over, perspiration breaking out on her skin from the sudden, dizzying fear that assailed her.

Dear heaven! Something was going wrong!

For a few moments she didn't know what to do, stemming her panic with a few deep, calming breaths. She felt sick and faint—more, she guessed, from fear than from anything else. But the dizziness—like her pain—was very real, even if it was purely emotional, and firmly she told herself it would be no good passing out in the office. She had to get home!

Buzzing through to her secretary, she managed to inform the girl in a cool, matter-of-fact voice that she still wasn't feeling well and would she call her a taxi? Consequently, she was able to leave the office with the minimum of fuss, although she wasn't able to fool a discerning Myrtle who came in with some shopping only seconds after Erica, and insisted on telephoning the doctor.

He arrived within minutes, and then, a little later, Rafe, and Erica looked at him with dark, wounded eyes as he came into the bedroom, tormented as much by the thought of his meeting Vikki yesterday as by what the doctor had just told her. Vaguely, she deduced that the housekeeper must have contacted him through his car phone—guessing he'd already be on his way back—although only afterwards did she consider the speed at which he must have driven to have got to her bedside so soon.

His eyes were hooded as they met the tortured depths of hers, but he was speaking to the doctor, the strong bones of his face seeming more prominent than usual under the olive skin. 'What is it? The baby?'

'Yes... but this pain she has...' The doctor turned to Rafe, his expression grave. 'I don't like it. I can't rule out the possibility of an ectopic. That's a——'

'I know what it is!' Rafe interrupted hoarsely, and Erica thought he winced just as she had done when Dr Lucas had told her. 'Good grief!' he whispered. 'That can be life-threatening...'

From the rigidity of his body she could see that he was shaken, and for a moment she wanted to reach out and touch him—find consolation in the physical strength of him—until she reminded herself, as she had when the doctor had first revealed his worst suspicions, of exactly why he had married her, that someone else had his affection, not her, and what losing this baby might mean...

'It will mean hospital... a termination of course...' It was the doctor's voice again and then Rafe's, cool, deep, disclosing nothing.

'Of course.'

'Although, depending upon how far things have gone...' Dr Lucas snapped his bag shut. 'You realise it could affect your wife's chances of getting pregnant again...'

'Yes.'

They were talking over her as if she weren't there—as if she weren't the one lying there sick at heart, as if it weren't *her* baby she was losing—only Rafe's...

'She needs to be admitted immediately.' Dr Lucas gestured towards the phone by the bed and, at Rafe's curt nod, started making the arrangements, that sense of urgency about him only adding to Erica's wretchedness—

her misery over losing the one thing she wanted more than anything else in the world. 'I think you'd better take her yourself, since you're only a stone's throw from the hospital. You do realise, though, that if it is an ectopic there's always the chance that there might be no more children for her in the future.'

Oh, heaven, how cruel it sounded!

'No more?' Rafe had gone deathly white. 'But surely...one ectopic...I thought that could leave a fifty-fifty chance...'

'If the worst comes to the worst—no. Not with that operation she had——' Dr Lucas stopped abruptly, the bewilderment on Rafe's face making him realise probably that he was overstepping the boundaries of confidentiality.

'Erica,' he said, with a disapproving glance at her where she lay, eyes dark and enormous in her small, pale face. 'I think there's something you should have told your husband, don't you?' And, scooping up his bag, he swept brusquely out of the room, leaving her alone to face the hard, interrogating emotion she saw in Rafe.

'What do you want to take with you?'

He wasn't asking any questions—intent only on getting her to the hospital—which was worse, she realised, because she wanted to tell him.

It wasn't until they were en route, though, weaving through the busy traffic, that he said, 'Well? What did Dr Lucas think you should have told me, Erica?' The eyes turned towards her were cool and gin-clear, mirroring a character that was frank and forthright, and would never have allowed him to lie to conceal a truth as she had done. Remorsefully, she swallowed before explaining.

'I was worried you'd refuse to help Dad if I'd told you,' she admitted, in conclusion, realising that that didn't really excuse her at all. Whichever way one looked at it, she'd been wrong not telling him at the beginning, and she'd often felt guilty, not owning up. Then, when, by some miracle, she had conceived almost immediately, she'd stopped feeling quite so deceitful—never dreaming that something like this might happen. And now she supposed it served her right . . .

'So that accounts for that scar you've always passed off as an appendectomy.' He sounded quietly annoyed—as he had every right to be, she thought, watching him steer the big car through the chaotic streets—control in every hard, nerveless inch of him. 'For heaven's sake, Erica! What sort of ogre did you imagine I was?' He exhaled a long breath, changing gear, saying almost to himself, 'And I'd always believed there was truth between us if nothing else.'

Heatedly, because, after all, he'd given her little choice about marrying him, she said, 'Wouldn't it have made all the difference to your offering that evidence—your insisting I marry you—if you'd known?'

Glacial chips of sapphire surveyed her so intently that he had to swerve to avoid another car that pulled out suddenly from a side-road, making him swear rather coarsely.

'What do *you* think?' he ground out.

She didn't answer—couldn't—but she knew. Why else would he have been so angry? He wanted a wife who would give him the children he expected, not some unproductive creature he didn't even love. And as the car turned into the hospital gates, the physical discomfort she was suffering was nothing compared with the gruelling, mental agony that seemed suddenly to be tearing her apart. A foolish, pointless heartache springing from the knowledge that, if she lost this baby through some freak act of Nature, then she'd almost certainly lose Rafe as well.

CHAPTER SEVEN

RAFE was waiting in the small private ward when Erica returned, her final tests completed.

'Well?' he asked quickly of the young nurse who accompanied her, an anxious furrow between his brows. 'Is it ... what the doctor suspected?'

The young girl grimaced. 'I think *you'd* better tell him, don't you?' she advised Erica, before removing an empty jug from beside the bed, and disappearing out of the room.

'Well?' he pressed, somewhat breathlessly this time.

Erica pulled the bedclothes up around her, meeting the concern in those deep blue eyes. 'They said it *was* a threatened miscarriage and that Dr Lucas was probably being cautious in view of my case history,' she started to tell him, then, 'although they think the chance of my miscarrying is greater than with most women ... so they said ... we'll have to be careful ...' She couldn't look at him, knowing that he understood exactly what she meant, wondering how he'd react to that, before she went on, 'Anyway, everything's still normal and where it should be,' and after the briefest of pauses, 'Your baby's fine.'

She sensed the tangible tension in him ease, heard him release his breath as if he'd been holding it too long, but her own relief choked her—just as it had when she'd been told she was still pregnant—and through the mist of her tears she saw Rafe frown.

'I don't believe it,' he whispered incredulously, the deepening lines around his eyes and mouth making him look oddly strained. 'You'd really rather be infertile than have my child, wouldn't you?'

Was that why he thought she was crying? Because she didn't want it? *Him?* How could he be so wrong? She wanted to tell him that it was because she had thought herself in danger of losing both, but she couldn't, and, sniffing back her tears, she glanced away from him, down at the still insignificant mound of her stomach, flinching from the quiet anger in his voice as he went on.

'Well, if you want to treat me like such a fiend, then, damn you, Erica! I'll start behaving like one. I shan't be giving you the satisfaction of that evidence—the only thing that matters to you, that you married me for—until you give me what *I* want. Our child.'

'Do anything you like!' she flung at him bitterly, sniffing again, grabbing at the clean white handkerchief he tossed down on to the bed.

'I intend to,' he said crisply, standing there with that dominant, male streak controlling him, those dark, arresting features grim with resolve. 'Whether you want this baby or not, it seems it wants to be born. And if it means cosseting you through every day of your pregnancy, I'm going to see that it is—and safely,' he concluded, so that she looked up, wondering what put that strange inflexion in his voice—that almost desolate look in his eyes. Was it pity for her? she thought wretchedly as she blew her nose, aching inside. 'That means no more working for you from now on——'

'But I—— '

'No buts,' he said peremptorily, cutting across her protests. 'There'll be a job for you at Witneys any time you want one, but in the meantime there'll be no more scares like this. I'm taking you away.'

She was about to ask where—put up some resistance—but suddenly she realised that she didn't want to. She wanted to go away. Though it hurt to admit it, she was under no illusion that Rafe's interest lay anywhere but with the welfare of his child, but, similarly, she had to admit that he was right. It was senseless to go on working even if there was only the slightest chance that doing so might cause her to miscarry, because, for whatever reason it had been conceived, she wanted this baby, she thought, with a fierce wave of emotion—even if Rafe believed otherwise—and she would do everything in her power to protect its innocent little life.

So quietly she murmured her acquiescence, and saw the surprise in those strong features chased away by relief when he obviously realised that she wasn't going to argue.

It was an early June day when they moved into Rafe's house in Scotland, a warm, bright day tempered by the last breezes of spring.

The square stone building stood at the head of a small loch, facing westwards across the water, its prospect of gentle green slopes pointing the way to the more austere crests of the barren mountains, the road leading to it some rarely used off-shoot of the main highway they had left a couple of miles back.

'It's beautiful.' Erica stepped out of the BMW, looking back across the gravel drive. Lawns on either side were hemmed with shrubs and flowering cherry trees; clumps of yellow alyssum and pale blue lobelia added touches of colour closer to the ground, while the land itself was fenced off from the banks of the loch by a low stone wall.

'It's more than that,' Rafe said quietly, closing the car door. 'It's home.'

Erica noted the satisfaction in his voice that told her it pleased him to be there—the place where he had said he had grown up, spent a happy childhood, she reflected, following him to the front door, wishing only that she could have been a wife he really wanted to bring here—the woman he loved.

'No,' he said, as she made to step inside, to her surprise catching her up in his arms and carrying her across the threshold.

She laughed, although his strength made her tremble, his intimate closeness filling her with an aching warmth, her cheeks with colour. He didn't seem to notice, however, kissing her lightly on the nose before setting her down again and, taking her hand, said brightly, 'Come on. I'll show you round.'

It was a pleasantly surprising tour, since Rafe seemed to have an amusing anecdote for every room they entered, from the sunny classically furnished lounge and the library, with its pink brocade suite and book-lined walls, to the comfortably decorated bedrooms and Victorian-style kitchen. Here a range took pride of place inside the inglenook fireplace, and a huge dresser displayed delicate china, gleaming from the sunlight streaming in from a dome-shaped conservatory beyond.

Myrtle had been invited to join them, her touch already apparent in the small herb pots decorating the windowsill, in the stocked cupboards and the shining brass furnishings beside the hearth. Myrtle had arrived just under a week ago, suggesting she make the place comfortable before they settled in, but she was spending today with her nephew in Glasgow, a discreet move, Erica realised, to allow her and Rafe time alone together—like newlyweds—in their equally new home. Which was rather pointless, she thought, with a sharp twinge of pain as she went over to the window, since Rafe hadn't made love to her—or even touched her in anything but an impersonal way—since that scare two weeks ago, his further intention not to made obvious by his recent complying with her earlier request for separate bedrooms. He wanted to safeguard his child's life. That was all he was interested in now, she realised, her eyes like two deep, dark pools set in the pale oval of her face. And what Myrtle made of such goings on, she wasn't sure, knowing that the housekeeper, for all her outspokenness, would have more diplomacy than to comment.

'What are you thinking about?' He had come up behind her, hands on either side of hers on the edge of the ceramic sink.

Erica stiffened in awareness, dangerously drawn to his warmth—that pleasant scent of him—like a bee to sweet, warm pollen.

'I was only wondering if there were any particular fish out there,' she lied rather tremulously, steering her thoughts towards something less disturbing, her gaze towards a mallard floating pompously out on the sunlit loch, its green head shimmering like a jewelled crown beside the drab brown plumage of its mate.

A smile touched Rafe's lips as if he didn't wholly believe her, but, stooping so that his dark head was on a level with hers, said, pointing, 'You see that small island out there towards the middle?' She nodded, her senses plunged into turmoil from his unbearable closeness— the sheer male vitality of him—though she remained outwardly calm. 'My grandfather had me fishing from that spot before I was three. Trout, salmon, pike—we caught them all. He used to say we were getting back to Nature—man pitting his wits against the fish to see who'd come out on top. It wasn't until I was older that I realised that it wasn't so much a sport as a long test of endurance. With man's superior brain, a boat and the ability to tie flies to look just like the real McCoy, the poor little devils really didn't stand a chance.'

Lips curving softly, she looked up into his eyes, her feeling for him reinforced. That was one of the reasons she so reluctantly loved him, she realised, because of that fairness in him—that appreciation of life. He'd never be deliberately cruel or waste life simply for pleasure. And yet he'd given very little regard to hers...

'...noticed the wall crumbling on the loch-side when we were coming in.' She heard his quiet observation as she lifted a small lavender plant off the tiled window-sill, ostensibly to inhale its fragrance, though in truth to hide the anguish in the tense contours of her face. 'We can't run the risk of junior coming to any harm when he starts toddling, can we?'

There was soft laughter in his remark, but his assumption, coupled with her own inner turmoil, had Erica dumping the little pot back on the sill rather aggressively, so that a sprinkling of dark soil fell out on to the ancient tiles.

'Aren't you rather presuming a lot?' she accused, golden flecks glittering in her eyes. 'Supposing it's a girl? Or will you drown it at birth if it is? Because *she* isn't going to carry your name on when she finally inherits my father's company, is she, and that's what you really want, isn't it?'

Something hard glinted in his eyes. But then, with a half-smile, he said, 'Who knows? She could well turn out to be one of these staunch, confirmed spinsters who hangs on to her career like the captain of a sinking ship and terrifies everyone else in sight.'

'Not if I can help it!' Erica returned indignantly, but the amusement that put tiny creases around Rafe's eyes was infectious, and she couldn't help laughing with him.

In fact, she was surprised to find herself laughing a lot over the following days—days when she almost forget the gulf that lay between her and Rafe, the real reason he had married her. As for the primary reason she had married him—for that evidence he was still with-holding—he seemed determined to wait until his child was born before he finally handed it over, and, though it was agony accepting it, she knew why. He despised her, still believing she'd thought him inferior to her all those years ago, and he was determined to extract payment from her in full. She wanted to tell him the truth. That she had loved him—still loved him! And that this baby was the most wonderful thing that had ever happened to her. She couldn't do that, though, because her pride wouldn't let her. He might even think she was just trying to get round him—declaring affection just to get that evidence out of him sooner—which would only make him despise her more, and she couldn't bear that. Then, on the other hand, he might believe her, and if he realised she loved him he might use her love as another weapon against her to hurt and humiliate her, or at the very most look at her with that pity she had seen in his eyes in the hospital...

'You're too pensive,' he commented, that first Sunday when they were in the larger and more rambling garden at the rear of the house. 'You're always too pensive. And carry on showering those cucumber plants like that and you'll have water melons instead!'

She laughed when she noticed the small puddles she was making around the dark green, sturdy little plants, and turned her sprinkler on to some unsuspecting young lettuces she had bought in the village earlier in the week, delighting in this sudden, new-found love-affair with the soil.

'The other day you mentioned our being here when the baby's toddling,' she reminded him, glancing to where he stood repairing a broken window-frame on the greenhouse. 'But I thought the idea of coming here was just to get away from London and my job—to make sure your child would have the best possible chance of survival——'

'*Our* child,' he corrected, tossing down a hammer, his long-limbed body moving lithely beneath his denim shirt and jeans. 'And the precautions were for both you and

the baby,' he stated, with a stray glance in her direction.
'Apart from which, I work quite happily from my
Dundee office.' A transition he had made in coming here
which was working well so far, alongside the days when
he flew down to London to complete his restructuring
programme of Witneys and check on things in his own
head office. 'What's wrong? Wouldn't you like to stay
on?' Looking out across the deep, placid loch to the
peaks of the silent mountains, Erica felt a strange com-
placency stir within her. The house here lacked the
modern opulence of the penthouse, and the classic luxury
of her father's Surrey home, but it had a grandeur all
its own. There was a pride and dignity in its architecture,
as if its very walls had imbibed the characters of the
proud Scots people who had lived within them, and she
loved it, experiencing a sudden, inexplicable feeling of
belonging. But, of course, she couldn't tell him that—
or even explain it to herself—and, transferring her hose
to play on a patch of freshly sown beetroot, she said
casually, with a little shrug, 'I don't mind. Whatever
you want.'

'Whatever I want?' He laughed, picking up the
hammer again and wielding it with a few positive strikes,
the sounds ringing back to them from the surrounding
hills. 'Now that's what I call a complaisant wife!'

'Is that what you think?' Erica's lips compressed in
mock rebellion, and a sudden, wicked gleam came into
her eyes. 'Well, get a load of this!'

With a swift tug on the sprinkler, she was training the
hose-pipe straight at him, thumb held hard over the
nozzle so that the water splayed out with maximum force,
catching him fully down one side.

'Don't you——!' He sprang out of the way, but she
moved too quickly, showering him again, her laughter
resounding over his desperate, aggravated shouts. 'Turn

it off! For God's sake, take it off me! Turn it off, or so help me I'll leather your backside if I come over there!'

Which he probably would, she thought recklessly, but he wasn't going to, and anyway, she was having too much fun, until she realised that he had stopped dodging the merciless spray and was coming—head down—straight for her, and then she dropped the hose with a wild shriek and darted off into the house.

She had only reached the kitchen before he caught her, and then he was the one who was laughing while she struggled futilely in his grasp.

'No, Rafe, please! No! Let me go!'

Like a wall of hard muscle behind her, he was urging her towards the sink, forcing her head down under the tap with probably every intention of turning it on, except that her pleading shrieks and his laughter brought Myrtle to the door, although, to Erica's surprise, the woman merely uttered, 'Oh, I'm sorry, sir,' and quickly made herself scarce.

'You see,' he grinned, releasing her from the threat of a retaliatory dousing. 'Even Myrtle thinks it best to leave you to my mercy, but I think I'll deal with you later. Perhaps that spanking might be more effective...'

His lips brushed her neck in a casual reprieve, though his touch was agony, especially when it lingered, his hard breathing broken as he inhaled the delicate scent of her skin.

Impelled by some instinct beyond her will, she leaned back against him with a small murmur, and just for a second felt the rigidity of his body beneath his damp clothes, heard the sudden, quick catch of his breath. But then he was pulling her hard into him, one arm locking across her breasts, his lips devouring, teeth nipping the heated skin of her throat, the rapaciousness of his kisses calling to a hunger in her that had her twisting her head to expose more of her flesh to the delicious ecstasy of his mouth.

As if she had conveyed some secret language to him, he responded to the need in her, slipping her blouse off one shoulder, lips moving fervently across the pale slope, seeking, stimulating, tasting the pure feminine honey of her body.

His hand slid down to rest against the still flat plane between her hips; she could feel its warmth through her pale cotton trousers, the gentle pressure of his fingers a silent communication to the child she carried for him, the gesture possessive, proprietorial, protective...

'Rafe,' she murmured softly, before his hands came up to cup her breasts. She gave a sharp, throaty gasp, feeling their instantaneous response that only assured him of her need of him as they swelled and blossomed beneath the hard caress of his palms.

Oh, heaven! She wanted him!

Desire pierced through her—poignant and sweet—and she uttered a small frustrated sound, reaching up to clasp his dark head to her fevered skin, wallowing in his pure, masculine scent, in the corded strength of his throat, so demented with need of him that she moved against him like some abandoned nymph, feeling she'd go crazy if he denied her now.

He pulled her round, and she could see the tension in his face, the dark flush suffusing his skin. Then his mouth clamped down on hers, hungry and devouring, as though he wanted to eat her alive, his passion feeding hers so that she *wanted*...

Suddenly the muscles in those strong arms flexed and he was drawing away from her, even before she had regained her senses enough to recognise the shrill ringing of the phone. He murmured some audible curse when Myrtle didn't pick it up, and Erica clutched at the sink for support as he went to answer it himself.

'That was Kirsteen,' he informed her tonelessly, coming back after a few minutes. And when Erica frowned, still battling with the sensations that had racked her a few minutes before, 'You remember—my cousin. You met her at the wedding. She wants us to drive over and have dinner with her this evening.'

Of course she remembered. She had a swift, mental reminder of the tall, dark-haired woman she had liked immensely, murmuring absently, 'That's nice,' alive to nothing at that moment but the intense, gnawing ache in her stomach, her eyes trained on his as if her silent supplication alone could bring him back into her arms.

But, of course, it couldn't. Wanting her though he had, it was plain now that he was relieved to have had that telephone call, the strong features composed once more, the passion that had ruled him now well under control. He hadn't intended making love to her. She knew that from the way he had tensed when she had surrendered to the first touch of his lips, and she knew she should have had more sense than to have encouraged him. She wanted to protect their child as much as he did, even if that was the last thing he believed about her. But he didn't know how much she wanted this baby— his baby—and she knew she could never tell him. Whatever he felt for her now, it certainly wasn't anything so sentimental as the depth of feeling that ravaged her constantly with the need for his tenderness, and so, with all the mental strength she could summon up, she made her voice sound casual enough to ask, 'Have you any suggestion what sort of thing I should wear?'

A faint smile touched his lips as his gaze tugged down over her, his appraisal cool and thorough as though he were weighing every nerve and cell susceptible to him, bringing warm colour to her cheeks, before he said, 'Whatever you wear, you'll look beautiful, but something casual will do.'

Taking his advice, she decided on some harem-style trousers in cerise silk with a matching full-sleeved blouse, pulling on casual sandals in the same shade, only breaking up the colour with a slim gold bangle and a narrow gold chain around her neck. Then, with the heavy blonde hair swept up, a few applications of mascara and a cerise lipstick created such a striking effect that it had Rafe audibly catching his breath when he saw her.

'You look like Aurora,' he said softly, those blue eyes burning with masculine appreciation and something else she couldn't quite define. 'Goddess of the dawn. Haloed in gold and promising untold delights for a new day...new life.' His gaze had slid to her midriff, dark lashes lowered, features complacent with a satisfaction at the child they had created, and Erica felt the sudden quickening throb of her pulse.

'Isn't there something about red in the sky at dawn?' She laughed lightly to ease her own tension, drawing Rafe's attention to the striking cerise that swathed her slender frame. 'Something about a warning...'

With teasing in her voice, she hooked her finger into a black jacket she'd left lying on a chair, and, with a provocative glance in his direction, tossed it over one shoulder and swept airily out to the car.

The evening was warm and still as she came out of the house, her sandals making a light tap over the steps. The sky was misty blue, tinged pink over the western edge of the loch. A light breeze stirred the red leaves of the chery trees, and from somewhere out on the water came the low-pitched rippling of a grebe.

'Are you intimating that I should be careful, Erica?' Rafe had followed her out, an unmistakable challenge in his eyes, and she gave him a demure smile as he opened her door, her heartbeat quickening as his arm casually brushed hers, her senses too aware of him, of the lean hardness of his body beneath the black shirt and trousers, of the proud, jutting lines of his profile.

'Well, you never know!' She laughed at him over the bonnet as he moved around to his own side of the car. 'Didn't this Aurora kidnap handsome men and then turn them into moths or something?'

'One in particular—and it was a grasshopper, actually. And I think I'm perfectly safe there.' The sound of his door closing echoed hers as he slid on to the seat beside her. 'You like wildlife too much to burden any poor, unsuspecting creature with a character like mine.'

She wasn't sure whether she'd imagined that self-censuring note in his voice, but she laughed again as he turned the key in the ignition, saying, 'There's always a first time for everything, so don't you be too sure!'

She loved this occasional banter with him—this hypothetical frivolity—which made her adrenalin flow, stimulating her both mentally and physically; but she wasn't fooling anyone. The dawn goddess might have had control over all *her* men, but in this partnership Rafe had the controlling hand—over her happiness, her emotions, her future.

The thought subdued her, and involuntarily she shuddered, realising just how vulnerable her love for this man made her, and how easily, therefore, he could destroy her. Consequently, when they arrived at the McBanes' she had lost some of her earlier sparkle, but nevertheless it was an enjoyable evening. Kirsteen and her happy-go-lucky husband, Doug, couldn't have been friendlier, in spite of having their hands full with Christopher and Lucy, their two young, active children, and a boisterous collie which spent most of the evening energetically savaging a discarded shoe.

'Rafe hasn't stayed in Scotland for any length of time since he left university,' Kirsteen told Erica, when they were in her large, disorganised kitchen, clearing away

the dishes after a delicious home-cooked meal. 'Uncle
Adam—Rafe's father—always came back here when he
could, even though he had a permanent home in London.
Rafe, though, has always been too much of a worka-
holic to take his finger off the pulse of his empire for
any length of time—until now.' She smiled at Erica as
she pressed the button to activate the dishwasher that
came to life with a sudden burst of energy, her friendly,
twinkling eyes not quite the deep blue of Rafe's. 'You
must bring out the homing instinct in him,' she commented in her warm, Scottish tones.

A little ache of emptiness gnawed at her insides. 'Oh,
I don't know about that,' she responded, rather too
wistfully she felt, longing, as she was, to be able to share
his cousin's opinion. But Kirsteen didn't know that Rafe
wasn't in love with her, and she couldn't let the other
woman suspect that she and her new husband weren't
completely happy, and so more lightly she went on, 'I
think he just felt that it was a desirable place to settle
—to start a family when the time comes.' It was some
time yet before her pregnancy would begin to show, and
she still hadn't told anyone other than Myrtle and her
father about the baby—didn't want to—almost afraid
that, if she did, something might go wrong. 'Besides, I
think he thought it was time I met his family properly,'
she added as a further diversion.

'What's left of us!' Kirsteen gave a little laugh as she
cling-wrapped the remains of the delicious coffee gateau
they had had for dessert. 'There's only me and mine and
another cousin up in Shetland whom both of us seldom
see. A family's important to him, though,' she en-
lightened Erica. 'As you probably know, his parents div-
orced when he was just a toddler, and his mother didn't
want to know. When both my parents died in a boating
accident when I was twelve—the year our grandfather
died—I went to live with Rafe and Uncle Adam where

you are now, so we were more like brother and sister really than cousins. I'd better hide this at the back of the fridge,' she remarked, grimacing down at the gateau, 'or the children will polish it off for breakfast in the morning.'

Erica smiled, thinking ahead to the day when she might find herself looking for devious ways to protect the interests of her own offspring—and her larder!—and a tide of warm feeling spread through her. There would be other things, too, like bedtime stories, and trips to the zoo, little cards that said, 'Love to Mummy', something that would make Christmases ahead so much more magical...

But would Rafe still be around to share the child's upbringing with her? After all, Kirsteen had said that a family was important to him. Or, she wondered, with a sudden sharp shattering of the dreams she'd been weaving, would he, having exhausted every possible use of her, leave her eventually for someone he really wanted to be with, someone who would have the love he had never given her? Like Vikki Stavros perhaps? The speculation tore at her so that it was a job conjuring up a smile as Kirsteen broke into her unhappy thoughts, suggesting they join the men.

They left the McBanes shortly afterwards, with their hostess making Erica promise to come and see them again.

'What did you think of them?' Rafe asked, as they were driving home.

Erica smiled, her earlier, unsettling thoughts pushed to the back of her mind. 'It was bedlam! But I liked it,' she admitted warmly, because, as a child, with only a father who, though caring, had often been too busy to give her much of his time, she'd sometimes felt as though she had missed out on a normal family life altogether. Consequently, she had loved the reigning chaos of the

McBanes, and reiterated as much to Rafe. 'I always wanted brothers and sisters,' she confessed wistfully. 'You were lucky having Kirsteen.'

He chuckled as he steered the BMW around the sweep of a wide loch, the powerful beam of his floodlights streaking across the surface of the deep, dark water. 'I suppose I was,' he said. 'We fought like cat and dog half the time, but woe betide anyone who tried to come between us or pick a fight with the other. Then we'd stick togther like chewing-gum to the sole of your shoe!'

'It sounds like fun,' she laughed.

'It was.' There was a moment's silence while she tried to imagine him as a grubby, squabbling schoolboy, but somehow couldn't quite visualise it. 'What about you?' He was glancing her way, then back at the road again. 'Didn't you have fun? I would have imagined the childhood you probably enjoyed would have been the type most kids would envy.'

'Why?' she quizzed, a little defensively. 'Because I was privileged? Well you're wrong. I couldn't make many friends at home because I was always away at school, and those I made there lived in other parts of the country so I seldom saw anyone of my own age during the holidays. Most of the time it was very lonely. I'd rather have been poorer and had a big family.'

Head averted, she felt the puzzling assessment of his eyes upon her. Then quietly, 'Does that mean Alecco was right?' She frowned, turning to see the hard, half-amused lines of his face. 'Does that mean you're going to fill my house with babies for me, Mrs Cameron?'

His tone gave little away, but he had to be far from serious. He believed this baby was the last thing she wanted, so he would hardly be expecting her to produce more! Pain cut into her when she thought of how happy she might have been—marrying and conceiving so easily when she had resigned herself to a childless future—

happy, perhaps, if she had been married to someone else? But no, she admitted hopelessly to herself. She would never have been happy in any other man's arms. Only Rafe's. He had been the only one for her from the very first moment of her sexual awakening. He had shown her how exquisite being a woman could be—and how painful. So she sat, tight-lipped, saying nothing in case her voice betrayed her, and when he looked at her she turned away, staring out at the inky blackness of the loch.

She heard him curse under his breath, then ram the car into a lower gear to take a sharp bend, and after that he drove with more aggression than usual for the rest of the way home.

CHAPTER EIGHT

JUNE slid into July, and August was upon them, and, as summer blossomed, so did Erica. Her pregnancy had put a bloom into her cheeks, added an extra lustre to her already shining hair, and now her condition was becoming very apparent, forcing her to accept that she needed some maternity wear, the morning Kirsteen made one of her customarily unexpected calls.

'Why didn't you tell me?' she exclaimed triumphantly, as one glance over Erica's burgeoning figure revealed the truth. 'How long have you known?' And without waiting for an answer, 'I'll kill Rafe—keeping a thing like this from his own family!'

Kirsteen was obviously beside herself with pleasure, so Erica had to smile. 'At first there were...problems, so we didn't want to say anything,' she responded, half truthfully, because she couldn't tell Kirsteen that this baby was anything but the happy outcome of two people who were desperately in love. But she was glad now to be able to talk openly about her baby, eager to share all the anticipation and excitement, and, despite everything, her secret personal joy she'd been nursing over the weeks, with another woman—someone who understood, adding with a laughing grimace as she tugged at the front of her restraining blouse, 'I'm going to have to get some new clothes!'

'Then let's do it now! There's no time like the present. I'll show you Perth, if you like. It's a lovely wee city. And I've bundled my two bairns off on an organised nature trail today, so I'm free for the next six hours!'

134

Kirsteen's enthusiasm fired Erica's, and suddenly a trip into town with a female companion sounded like fun.

'Give me five minutes,' she said, and went to get ready.

It proved to be a lovely day. Kirsteen's knowledge of the little market-type town helped to make shopping more of a joy than a tiring necessity, and Erica warmed to her new cousin-in-law as to a sister. They had a light lunch in a hotel restaurant from where they could see the river, and then afternoon tea in a contrasting little café which they found nestling among the shops. They chatted incessantly, about everything from child care and Scotland to Erica's job at Witneys, with Kirsteen telling her, while they were driving back, about the interior decorating business which she and Doug had started as newly-weds before Christopher had come along and put paid to all their plans, leaving Doug working mainly on his own.

'You'd never guess he was in that line—looking at our house!' she laughed, as Erica brought the Mercedes into the drive. She had insisted on taking her car—brushing aside the other woman's concern that she might overtax herself—guessing that as Rafe's cousin spent much of her time driving back and forth between school, music lessons and cub meetings, she would welcome the break. Silently, though, she had to admit to feeling a little weary, but she also felt happier than she had for some time, and she had a lot of satisfying purchases to show for her day out, too.

'Thanks for driving,' Kirsteen expressed, declining Erica's offer of a cup of tea. 'I really must get back and pick up the wee ones. It was nice to talk to another woman about something other than nappy rash and teething troubles, though. Thanks a lot. It's been a great day. Love to Rafe!' she called out, waving to Erica as she started the large estate car and pulled away.

Erica consulted her watch. It wasn't yet six. Rafe was never home before seven, and Myrtle had gone into Glasgow and wasn't expected back until much later. Consequently, she stopped dead in her tracks when she went inside and Rafe appeared in the hall.

'You're early,' she said breathlessly, pleased to see him, the pull of that powerful, male magnetism affecting her as it always did. He was still wearing his dark business suit, but the top of his shirt was unfastened, and his tie was pulled loosely askew revealing the sinewy strength of his throat.

'Where have you been?' He smiled, looking hot and rather tired, as if he had had a hard day. And with a cursory glance at her purchases, 'Shopping with Kirsteen?'

Of course. He'd seen the car, she realised, guessing he had already garaged his own, which was why she had thought he wasn't home.

'Yes.'

Wearily, he massaged the back of his neck, a dark sleeve pulling in resistance. 'Where did you go?'

She told him, and one black eyebrow shot upwards. 'You didn't drive all that way yourself, did you?'

'I'm quite capable——' she started, but he cut in, eyes narrowing into slits.

'And Kirsteen let you?'

'For goodness' sake! I'm not an invalid,' she contended, his sudden change of mood with her own fatigue making her snap more than she realised as she swung away from him into the lounge. 'I'm perfectly all right!'

'Yes, you look it!' he said sarcastically, following her. 'I would have thought, in view of what nearly happened before, you would have had more bloody sense!'

His anger was a palpable thing and, dumping her bags down on to a chair, Erica pivoted to face him.

'I'm not a child! And don't swear at me,' she protested tiredly, flinching from his temper that had burst into life like an unexpected storm.

'I'll speak to you any way I damn well please, if it will ram some logic into that senseless little brain of yours!' Lean hands pushed back his jacket, his chest flexing with anger, while Erica's throat worked nervously, her eyes glittering with retaliatory fire. 'What are you trying to do—see how far you can push yourself? Supposing you'd started a miscarriage on the road today?' And after the slightest hesitation, 'Or is that really what you were hoping for?'

She knew he was over-reacting, but that last remark tore through her, bringing hurt, angry colour into her cheeks.

If that was what he believed, then what was the point in trying to convince him otherwise? she thought torturedly, retaliating unthinkingly with, 'And what if I had been? What would you do about it, Rafe?' She couldn't help the taunt, wanting to hurt him as much as she was hurting inside. 'Slap a court injunction on me? That would look rather ridiculous, wouldn't it, when I told them how you got me to marry you in the first place? So how would you stop me, Rafe?'

For a moment she thought he was going to strike her. A dangerous glint had turned his eyes to ice, hands clenched at his sides. But his control was greater than she gave him credit for, because his voice was quite steady, although there was a bleakness to the strong, male features as he said, 'If I thought you meant that, I'd let you go now,' adding in more husky tones, 'Well? *Did* you mean it, Erica?'

She wanted to say yes, accept the chance to extricate herself from this painful entanglement with him, but she loved him too much to let him believe that she could be

capable of such a thing, destroy that part of herself—
that part of him—that was the only thing they really
shared, and miserably she shook her head.

He seemed to catch his breath. 'Then why are we
fighting?' he said quietly.

She could almost have believed there was pain in those
penetrating eyes, a raw desolation she knew she had to
be imagining even as her heart responded, her tortured
gaze locking with his, so that she answered tremulously,
'I don't know.'

One step, and he had closed the distance between them,
the light touch of his hand against her cheek tugging her
breath painfully from her lungs. She angled her head
into his caress, her lips making accidental contact with
his fingers, and she heard his swift inhalation, felt the
thunder of his heart beneath her palms. Her heart seemed
to leap out of control as he caught her to him—wanting
her—the strong arms around her flexing in an agonising
hold as one hand stroked the shining gold mantle of her
hair. Her face against his shoulder, she breathed in his
glorious warmth—his scent—a husky murmur of need
escaping her lips. But he was putting her from him, his
eyes dark and hooded, every inch of him taut from the
effort of that reasoning self-discipline, although a faint
smile tugged at his mouth, and, with a wry glance
towards the bags she had brought home, he said softly,
'Are you going to show me what you bought?'

She didn't want to. She wanted to stay in his arms.
Oh, heaven, for him to make love to her! But she knew
he wouldn't. He valued his child's life too much for that.
Which, of course, was the most important thing to her,
too—her baby's safety. But even so, it was difficult
hiding her disappointment, her agonising frustration
from him as she did as he suggested, somewhat half-
heartedly at first, and then with growing enthusiasm as

Rafe made little comments of approval about her purchases. There were two dresses in blue and red jersey for the cooler winter months nearer the birth; a couple of blouses and some trousers. She had bought some material, too, with all the necessary filling to make a little quilt for the cot, and there was the little white toy kitten for the baby that she hadn't been able to resist, realising that it was still early days yet, but determined that her child would be born strong and healthy, which was one of the reasons why Rafe's suggestion that she didn't want it had hurt her so deeply. He didn't make any comment when he noticed these last two items, and his expression was shuttered so that she couldn't tell what he was thinking.

He left her then, going upstairs to change, but later when she was relaxing in the bath she heard him talking on the extension in the adjoining bedroom, and guessed from the distinct reprimand in his voice that he was having words about that afternoon with his cousin.

She should have listened to Kirsteen when she'd advised her not to drive, Erica thought with a grimace, wondering if the other woman had anticipated this sort of reaction from Rafe. Well, at least *she* had taken the worst of his temper and not Kirsteen, she reflected gratefully, experiencing a rare contentment as she sank down into the scented foam, because, listening to those deep, remonstrative tones coming from the other room, it was almost possible to imagine that he had acted as he had because he cared.

The next morning she awoke with a bilious attack just as Rafe was leaving for work, whereupon Myrtle immediately called him back into the house and telephoned for the doctor.

'Everyone makes so much fuss—I'm all right,' Erica stressed when the doctor had gone. Already she was beginning to feel better. 'Myrtle just panicked, Rafe. Honestly!' Her eyes lifted to the ceiling. 'If I weren't having a baby, no one would think anything of it.'

'Nevertheless, lass, he has told you to stay in bed.' Hands on hips, disapprovingly, Myrtle viewed the pale features looking back at her from the bed before sending an imploring glance towards her employer. 'Really, sir...' Her tone appealed. 'I wish you'd make her take more care of herself. I came back from the village the other day and found her perched on the step ladder outside taking down that old bird box by the conservatory.'

Trust Myrtle to tell him that! She noticed the silently dismissing glance he gave the housekeeper, and deliberately avoided looking at him as he closed the door quietly behind her, keeping her gaze on the coffee satin of the duvet as he came back to the bed and sat down, one arm on either side of her.

'You know what I ought to do to you, don't you?' he breathed, his words softly promising something she knew he'd never carry out. He looked devastating, as always, in his dark suit—elegant, sophisticated and hard—that potent maleness with the heady scent of his cologne calling to everything that was feminine in her.

'Well, I wanted the blue tits to have a clean place to nest in the spring... and you aren't always here,' quietly she pointed out, lowering her gaze, suddenly embarrassed that that might have sounded like a plea to him to spend more time with her, which, if she were truthful with herself, it was.

Strong fingers curled around her chin, bringing her gaze back to the merciless regard of his. She felt a rush of colour in her cheeks as the fine contours of her face were open to his searching assessment. Then he said softly, 'Well, we'd better do something about that, hadn't we?'

He did, immediately, taking the day off work to look after her himself, instead of leaving her to the despairing Myrtle. He brought her lunch on a tray, sitting with her while she ate, and afterwards he spent the afternoon catching up on some bookwork, half reclining on the bed, while she read a magazine, oddly content in the amiable silence that engulfed them. Once she dozed, waking to feel the hard warmth of him still pressing against her, and contentedly she dozed off again, re-assured that he was still there, feeling closer to him then than she had ever felt to anyone in her life.

After that, their relationship improved considerably. Rafe, though, still imposed total restraint upon any in-timacy between them, so that often she lay awake at night, aching for him, praying that he would come to her, if only to hold her, soothe her to sleep with the comfort of his warm, hard body, but she knew he would never have trusted himself to sleep with her. He might not love her, but she knew that, physically, he still wanted her, just as she wanted him. But he was aware that any intimacy between them might possibly risk the life of the child he'd been determined she would give him, just as she knew she should have been glad that he had chosen to leave her alone so that there was very little chance of his discovering her feelings for him. But she wasn't, and her need of him grew daily with the baby inside her, so that sometimes it was almost more than she could bear.

She began to wonder if her expanding figure made it easier for him to ignore her as a woman, if he might have started to look twice at the attractive young women she'd noticed once during a brief visit to his office. Or worse. The thought rose in her mind, torturing and cruel. Was he perhaps seeing Vikki—finding solace with the beautiful Mediterranean girl when he took those regular trips to London?

She refused even to give head-room to that unbearable suspicion, consoling herself with the reminder that he was at home far more often nowadays than he used to be.

He made changes around the place, too—alterations they had decided on together—which included putting finishing touches to the delicate pastel décor of the nursery, a room they had chosen for its sunny outlook and which now waited, like her, in happy expectancy of its little occupant. Sometimes, she felt, she could have been truly happy if she could have shared the real joy of her coming child with Rafe. But for that he would have to have loved her, and he didn't, painfully she had to force herself to remember when she became too fanciful and preoccupied with the wonderful thing that was happening to her body. They wanted this baby for different reasons. He, merely because he wanted an heir—and from her. It was as unemotional and cold-blooded with him as that—a way of forcing her to accept him and his Cameron blood into Witneys, and so make her pay for the way he thought she had treated him five years ago. She, on the other hand, welcomed it with all her desperation to have a part of a man she was hopelessly in love with—perhaps the only part of him she would ever have—the vain hope to which she clung, that one day he might love her again as he had loved her in the past, dying like the summer when he remained only the courteous companion who shared her home.

Then, one mellow, autumn morning, she received a letter from Graham. He still bore a grudge, she realised at once, when the letter began: 'I wouldn't be writing to you, only I need some advice which unfortunately only you can give me,' then went on to request details about a customer with whom she had had personal dealings at Witneys.

Finishing her breakfast, alone, as Rafe had already left for the day, Erica bit back annoyance as Graham reiterated, in writing, the spiteful insinuations he had made before. 'Your father says you're pregnant. Now isn't that a surprise? Still, you didn't have to do the old-fashioned thing and marry him, did you? Didn't you ever consider for one moment what your marrying him did to me?' The whole tone of the letter changed then, making her realise that Graham was trying to convince himself, and her, that he was the totally abandoned lover, when in fact he had been nothing of the sort. And he was still implying that she had married quickly because she had been pregnant. Well, was she going to tell *him*!

Fetching some writing paper from the library, she started to dash off a letter there and then, screwing it up after she'd scribbled one or two angry lines and starting again, until after three attempts she realised what a pointless and childish exercise it was retaliating in such a way, deciding that the most effective course would be to ignore Graham's personal comments entirely, replying only with the necessary information for which he had asked. The only thing was, she had used up all the plain notepaper, she discovered, when she went back to the bureau, the only other being Rafe's company's headed paper which wouldn't have done at all. In the end, she settled for some rose-coloured stationery that her secretary had given her for her last birthday, and which was, rather disconcertingly, slightly perfumed.

Well, it would have to do, she thought, sitting down to write her letter in the sunny conservatory instead of using the typewriter on Rafe's desk, as it was such a lovely day, after which she sealed it in one of the matching, pink envelopes and took it upstairs, popping it into her handbag to post when she next went into the village. Then, with her offer to help Myrtle with the washing up firmly declined, she returned to the conservatory to work on her little duvet, smiling down at the pale lemon of her handiwork with a tranquil pleasure soothing away all her other worries as, almost in response, she felt the baby kick inside her.

It was at times like this, she thought, that she could almost pretend everything was perfect—when her child made her so vibrantly aware of its existence. Before she had conceived she could never have believed it possible to feel such an affinity with another human being—this depth of feeling for an unborn baby that was instinctive and beautiful and all part of the wonderful miracle of motherhood. She knew she looked good, too, all the joy she felt in her pregnancy extending to her physical wellbeing so that her eyes positively sparkled with health these days, her skin and hair exhibiting a flawless beauty she wasn't even aware of as she sat, immersed in a cocoon of contentment, poring over her labour of love.

Myrtle's nephew arrived at about eleven to take his aunt out for the day, a tall, strapping Scotsman, built like a heavyweight, whom Myrtle introduced as Malcolm, and who eyed Erica with a hot-blooded male fervour before complimenting her upon her needlework in a Glaswegian accent so thick she barely understood a word.

Once during the morning someone called collecting for the school fête in the village, and Erica chatted to the woman for a few minutes, wondering afterwards whether her child would ever attend the school to which she had just donated—wondering what the future would hold.

Looking that far ahead depressed her, and, having little appetite for the cold lunch Myrtle had left her, she went out into the garden to prune a few shrubs, feeling as lonely suddenly as the solitary gull she could see soaring above the loch, its plaintive cry drifting back to her on the fresh breeze.

'Rafe.' She whispered his name on a surge of foolish longing, shivering as the wind penetrated her soft, brushed cotton blouse. Secateurs in hand, suddenly she glanced up again, hearing a car making light work of the stretch of road up from the loch.

'Rafe!' It was the BMW she had heard, and eagerly she moved across the lawn as it purred into the drive, stopping in front of the house.

Strange how even the sight of him could make her pulse throb, she thought absently, her gaze following the elegant movements of the man as he got out of the car. There was an eye-catching sophistication in every small gesture, in the tilt of his dark head, in the sure confidence of his stride, in the firm, sensual mouth that was quirking now in wry amusement at her all too apparent pleasure at seeing him.

Dear God, I love him! It was an effort not to run to him and throw her arms around him, but she managed to stem the urge, thrusting her hands into the pockets of her trousers, calling out with feigned casualness, 'What are you doing home?'

His shoes crunched the gravel as he came over to her, his lop-sided smile causing her stomach to somersault. 'I remembered Myrtle was going out. I thought you might not like being left alone.'

How had he known? She hung on to his words as if they were rare gems, comparing his purity of speech— that hint of Celt that gave an arresting roundness to his vowels—with the rough brogue of the man she had met earlier. It was the first thing about him she had fallen in love with—his voice—she remembered, colour seeping into her cheeks as she murmured tremulously, 'Can I get you something to eat.'

'No, I'll have something later.' He glanced up at the sky, 'I thought I'd make the most of this sunshine and finish the pointing job on that wall.'

It was like being a normal married couple, she couldn't help thinking later, listening to the slow scrape of his trowel between the stones. She was planting next year's spring bulbs in the little border beneath his new stonework—crocuses, daffodils and irises—trying to ignore the little voice inside her that kept reminding her that they were anything but a normal couple, of the real reason he had married her—of the cold uncertainty of the future.

'You're quiet,' he remarked suddenly, on his haunches, his trowel still working while he glanced at her from a few feet away.

'Am I?'

'What are you thinking?'

She swallowed, unable to meet his eyes, pulling some weeds to clear a space for some pansies she was putting in. There was a pyracantha, too, that she intended to plant, to add a touch of colour to the garden with the pansies when the winter came and all the other flowers had withered.

'Nothing,' she lied, because she couldn't tell him the truth.

'Nothing?' He rested both arms on the low wall, giving her his full attention now, that keen regard too perceptive, too tuned to her every change of mood.

'I was thinking what a perfect job you've made on the wall—what a master builder you are!' She laughed, because she had been, marvelling at how capable he was. He wasn't above doing any menial task himself, and it was just another thing about him which made her admire him, she realised reluctantly, adding with another, tighter little laugh, 'My husband will be pleased!'

'No, you don't!' He had seen her pick up the spade, and immediately he left the pointing job he was doing, coming over to dig the small hole she needed for her pyracantha. His sleeves were rolled up, his sinewy forearms exposed, and Erica felt her throat contract from the sheer maleness of him, noticing the way his dark hair fell across his forehead as he worked, the movement of those hard muscles in his back beneath the khaki shirt.

Deftly, he finished the whole task, his strong, lean hands compressing the soil around the little shrub, and, standing up, he rubbed them on the rough brown cords he was wearing, saying with teasing in his eyes, 'There you are, Mrs Cameron. Shall I send your husband the bill? Or would you prefer to settle with me yourself before I go?'

It was a flippant quip, made in response to her own little jest, but suddenly the air seemed charged with electricity. She knew she should have pulled herself free of its influence, but she didn't want to, responding with a little tremor, 'What sort of price did you have in mind?' It was a dangerous game and she knew it, but she seemed compelled to keep on playing.

'Give me your hands.'

She frowned, but complied, blonde hair falling forward as she looked down at them in his, while he peeled off the rubber gloves that encased them with a sound like twin whips on the air. She went to pull away from him then, but he caught her, laughing softly as one strong arm wound itself around her distended midriff, pulling her back against him.

'Now, Mrs Cameron . . .' His lips were a tender caress against her hair. 'What time did you say this husband of yours was coming home?'

The fresh, outdoor scent of him, with the sudden sensation of his mouth against the nape of her neck, made her suddenly weak, her blood course through her as he turned her round in his arms, her hands meeting the solid muscle of him through the khaki shirt. Desire manifested itself as the ruling passion as his lips feathered kisses across her cheek and jaw, her mind striving to hold on to the last shred of her sensibilities.

'No, Rafe.'

Her breathless protest brought him to look at her, tongue clicking disapprovingly, one eyebrow arched in mock enquiry as though he didn't recognise the name. He was still playing this game they had started—pretending—though there was nothing imaginary about that fierce hunger that darkened his eyes. He dipped his head then, claiming her mouth with a bruising pressure that brought a small sound from her throat, and with her hands sliding up she curled her fingers into the hard bone of his shoulders, her passion rising to his.

They were two different people in this game they were acting out—two people with mutual needs and demands—each answering the other without any loss of pride on either part while they could forget who they really were, all reserve gone, swamped now by the driving needs of both of them, of man for his equal mate.

'Oh, yes, yes...' She arched her back as his lips moved over her throat to the generous cleft between her breasts, moving, burning through the fabric of her blouse and bra to the full swollen mound beneath. 'Oh, please...' Her nails dug deeper into the hard muscle of his shoulders, her body responding instinctively to the heady torture of his mouth.

He tugged her blouse free of her trousers, his earth-stained hands rough and warm against her bare flesh, moving with breath-catching deliberation to the heavy, aching roundness of her breasts.

'Oh, Rafe...' It was a soft murmur, barely audible, lost in the heat of her desire.

He pulled her to him then—fiercely, possessively—murmuring his appreciation of her warm pliancy beneath his hands, and, with his lips buried in the scented gold of her hair, he groaned raggedly, 'For goodness' sake, Erica, touch me!'

She didn't need a second invitation—wanting to—her fingers unsteady as she slipped the buttons of his shirt, the warm wall of his chest and that crisp, dark hair beneath her palms an electric stimulus to her own heightened arousal.

'Supposing someone comes?' She whispered it against the stirring heat of him, her tongue trailing wantonly down the warm length of his breastbone, tasting the salt on his skin, breathing in the elusive sweetness of his cologne with the more intimate scent of his body, knowing they were in full view of the road, but unable to care.

'No one will.'

His certainty reminded her that the road changed to a track a little way beyond the house, which meant no vehicles passed unless they had lost their way, and with the holiday season over the hikers—a regular sight during the summer months—were now few and far between.

'You're perfect,' she breathed, her hands moving lovingly down over the firm muscles of his back, delighting as she felt them flex beneath her fingers, felt his whole body tensing as she explored the tapering structure of his torso to the belt at his lean waist, the sight and scent and feel of him feeding her senses until his hand clamped down on hers and he said hoarsely,

'Let's go inside.'

She didn't remember afterwards whether she'd walked or whether he had carried her, only that she was in his arms when he laid her down on the bed, although when he went to move away to wash his hands she uttered a small groan of protest, tugging at his sleeve, so that he dropped down beside her with a twist of a smile.

'You're kinky,' he scolded softly, trailing a finger along the silken valley of her breasts, leaving a dark smear on her skin—against the white lace of her bra.

She shut her eyes to the probing sapphire of his, not caring what he thought, racked with a need too desperate to let him go even for a second—afraid that he wouldn't come back to her—helping him as he tugged at her blouse and bra and breathing a deep, shuddering sigh as his hands caressed the aching firmness of her breasts.

His palms were rough from the work he had been doing, stimulating the sensitive peaks with an exquisite torture that made her bite down on her lower lip to stop herself crying out the wanting inside of her. His clothes were rough, too, the coarseness of his shirt arousing on her soft skin, the buckle of his belt digging into her midriff. But when he removed them, and then the rest of hers, she was suddenly shy, acutely self-conscious, when she saw him gazing down at her, of how changed her figure was since he had last seen her like this.

'You're beautiful.' His words were breathed with almost reverential awe, and surprise and relief chased away the anxiety in her face so that she gave him a meek, tentative smile.

'Do you mean it?' She couldn't believe he did, when she had never thought of herself as such—and even less so now.

He didn't answer, instead moving to press his lips against the full curvature of her abdomen, his hands caressing the mound that enclosed his child as if it held the earth's riches, the hard structure of his face softened by something that tugged at her heart-strings, had her closing her eyes to blot it out for fear of crying out her love for him.

He took her then, obliterating everything else but the feel of him inside of her, the weeks of frustration and despair dispelling with a relief that burst with a shuddering cry from her lips. She sensed the restraint in him though—his consideration for her and the baby—despite his own, urgent need for release. And then it came, a slow-building, earth-shattering crescendo that had him clasping her back against him, taking her with him on a sensual journey of sensation, a heady, dizzying oblivion where there were only the two of them, where sensation turned into emotion that left her gasping and sobbing as he collapsed against her with a deep, throaty utterance of her name.

She was crying uncontrollably, face buried in the pillow, sobs shaking her body. He moved swiftly, sitting up, resting on an elbow as he turned her back to him, his skin slick with sweat, his face a blur of bewilderment as he stared down at her dark, wet lashes, the damp flush of her cheeks.

'Why in heaven's name are you crying?'

He sounded perplexed, almost quietly angry, but she couldn't tell him that it was he who had wrung that depth of emotion from her, that the release and fulfilment she had found in their lovemaking with the intensity of her love for him had all proved too much to hold inside, overflowing and spilling out of her like the bounties of a cornucopia.

Battling for control, she heard the bed squeak as he moved away from her, the absence of his warm body leaving her like one bereft.

'Why, Erica?' He was fastening the belt of his navy-blue robe, patting his hip pocket with a futile gesture as she sniffed back her tears. 'Have you got a handkerchief?'

'In the drawer,' she was about to say, but he had already found the box of tissues on the dressing-table, tugging a few out impatiently enough to send her handbag beside it toppling off the edge. He uttered a small oath, stooping to retrieve its scattered contents, his broad back stiffening as he straightened again, and with heart-sinking dismay Erica realised why. He was looking at Graham's signature on the letter that had fallen out, digesting the contents of that last, paradoxically lovelorn paragraph, and viewing the unfortunately perfumed envelope that contained her innocent reply.

'Rafe, I...' Pulling the duvet up around her, she started to explain, but was stalled by the flint-hard query burning in his eyes.

'I see.' He came towards her, his face a taut mask, every masculine muscle and sinew rigid with accusation. 'Is it regret that's making you cry, Erica? Making love with the wrong man? What did you do—whip up some enthusiasm by pretending I was Caddis? Or are you so frustrated for him that any man would have done?'

His mood was so frightening that she edged back against the headboard, pale hair cascading over one shoulder, the duvet barely concealing the creamy swell of her breasts.

'You would think that, wouldn't you?' she flung at him bitterly, eyes wounded from the brutal way in which he had destroyed something she had thought was mutual and beautiful between them. 'Why don't you read it all—and the reply?' she invited, her tone hurt and censuring, and realised he had taken it as a sarcastic taunt rather than a desperate plea to make him understand, when he uttered a curt, harsh laugh.

'No, thanks!' Dismayed, she watched as he screwed up Graham's letter and hurled it across the room. 'I don't get my kicks out of reading other people's love-letters—particularly those from my *wife's* lover!'

'He isn't my lover! He never was!' she shot back heatedly, two bright spots of colour staining the skin across her cheeks. 'You know better than that, Rafe,' she reminded him more calmly, and, her thoughts going back to that little house in Greece, added, with a small tremor, 'At least . . . I thought you could tell.'

His lashes lowered to veil his eyes so that she couldn't see what was in them, and with a swift, contemptuous gesture he tossed the rosy envelope down on to the bed.

'Yes.' His chest expanded with a long breath. 'So why?' he interrogated, thrusting his hands into his pockets, the muscles of his strong, hair-cased legs taut below the robe. 'Why didn't you sleep with him before, if you wanted him so much?' Roughly, he caught her chin as she would have turned away, his thumb biting into her flesh. 'Why, Erica?'

His eyes demanded an answer, and she swallowed from the dominating maleness of him, remembering how those earth-stained hands had driven her mindless for him, and, with a pulse fluttering erratically at the base of her throat, she met his gaze levelly to say with unerring truthfulness, 'Because I never wanted him as I wanted you.'

He inhaled sharply, his hand falling away from her. 'I see,' he said, his face impassive, though there were weary lines about his eyes, around his mouth. 'So at least it's me you're sharing the bed with.' There was a hard implacability to his words. 'Is that why you despise me, Erica, because of what I can do to you even though

I took you away from the man you really wanted? Well, don't worry, darling,' he went on before she could utter a word, 'I've found it to be a pretty good substitute, and in the long run a far more loyal bedfellow than all your idealistic fantasies of love.'

She had been about to say that she didn't despise him, but that last cynical remark cut her to the quick. If she had been wishing she could convince him there was nothing between her and Graham, she was glad now that she hadn't, realising, as he slammed into the bathroom, that if he still thought she was in love with another man, then he would never be likely to guess at her humiliating love for him. Pain ripped through her, making it difficult to breathe as, cruelly, she made herself accept that if he was hurt at finding that supposed love-letter, then it was only his pride that was wounded—nothing more.

After that, Rafe spent more and more time away from home, when he was there the climate between them almost unbearably cold.

Christmas came, bringing with it—among the many others—a card from Alecco and Maria Stavros, with Vikki's name included as a matter of course. Erica wasn't sure whether or not the other woman had returned to Greece for the holiday, but either way the card would obviously have needed to be posted long before then to avoid the seasonal delay. Perhaps Vikki had instructed her aunt to include her, even when she was still in England, wanting things to appear as innocent as possible, Erica thought resentfully, the vision of another, more intimately worded greeting sent to Rafe personally at his office torturing her still further, so that she had to draw the reins on her cruel imagination.

She was glad when the New Year was upon them and she could get away from the tense atmosphere of her own home in accepting her father's invitation to spend a few days in Surrey. Rafe drove her down, staying on himself for a couple of days before making the long journey back to Scotland. It was the change Erica needed, finding the familiar surroundings of her old home—the gentle walks along the fringes of her father's beloved and adjoining golf-course—took her mind away from the problems of her marriage.

'Well, you certainly look more relaxed than when you arrived,' Sir Joshua commented observantly on her last morning when she was waiting for Rafe to collect her. 'Has it been a difficult pregnancy, love?'

Glancing away from those paternal eyes, she bit her lower lip, wondering what to say to satisfy that shrewd, enquiring mind without having to lie, because it hadn't been, really. Fortunately, though, a maid came in to announce Rafe's punctual arrival, so that, thankfully, she was spared from having to answer.

'Well? Did you miss me?' he asked, though not without a trace of sarcasm when they were motoring back, and it was another question which she didn't know how to answer because she had missed him—dreadfully—and yet she'd been glad of the break, too. But he mistook her hesitancy in replying for a negation, she realised hopelessly a moment later, because he was rasping back at her across the plush interior of the car, 'Oh, no, I forgot. Caddis is almost a neighbour, isn't he? Why would you miss your husband when you've got an adoring boyfriend so close to hand?'

She didn't respond, refusing to be drawn into some banal and pointless argument with him, and she sank back into her seat, staring desolately out at the leafless trees and the forlorn-looking cattle in the fields that hemmed the motorway, feeling the old, strained atmosphere settling over her again like a dark cloud.

* * *

Things didn't improve, and one morning, during the following week, she awoke with such a depression that the only way she could shrug it off after Rafe had left for work was by forcing herself to do a little light sorting out of some cupboards.

The church in the village had sent round a notification of a coming jumble sale, requesting anything she might have to contribute, and, remembering the curtains she had taken out of the nursery and put away in the chest in the spare bedroom, Erica went up to get them.

They were a good quality cotton, and in perfect condition, too—she'd only taken them down because the bright, bold prints hadn't gone with the nursery's softer décor, she remembered, pleased to be able to offer the church something worthwhile. But as she lifted the heavy fabric out of the drawer, something fell back in with a soft rustle, so that she only noticed it then—the paper bag that had opened to spill the blue, cube-shaped jeweller's box—and something else. A small, scrap of paper that made her throat suddenly clog, her heart beat uncontrollably fast.

Laying the curtains down on the bed, she turned back to the drawer, her fingers trembling so much it was an effort to open the little box. It contained a man's watch— gold and elegant—the engraving she saw on the back when she lifted it out dragging a strangled sob from her lips. 'To my dearest love'. And there was no doubt who it was from, even though her tears blurred the bold initial at the bottom, because of that small scribbled note that had assured her as soon as she'd seen it that the little box held no surprise gift for her—a note that had read simply, 'Treasure it. Vikki'.

Her breath seemed to cut like knives through her lungs. So it was true! What more evidence did she need than that?

Stuffing the box back into the bag, she rammed the drawer closed, her breath coming quickly, hot tears scalding her cheeks. Had it been Vikki's Christmas gift to Rafe—an expensive declaration of her love engraved in gold? And if so, what had he given her in return? she wondered torturously. His undivided attention for a week and the pleasure of his bed, knowing his wife was safely installed in Surrey? Surely, they wouldn't have missed an opportunity like that?

A sob shook her slender body as she pictured the lovely Greek beauty in her husband's arms. She couldn't bear it! Oh, dear heaven, she couldn't!

She didn't think she could stay in that day and would have taken herself off for a long drive if she could have eased herself comfortably behind the wheel of the Mercedes. But that was out of the question and, feeling trapped in her desolation, gratefully, she accepted Malcolm's invitation, when he called, to join him and Myrtle on their weekly shopping trip—glad of anything that would take her mind off that cruel discovery of the morning, though nothing, not even friendly company, really helped. Then, on the way back, Malcolm started asking questions about the baby, laughing when she said that she and Rafe hadn't yet decided on a name.

'He's a lucky chap,' he commented, with an appraising male glance over her heavily fertile body. 'Some people have got it all.'

Unable to say anything, Erica looked away, out of her window at the dusky, passing countryside, brittle with a frost that had refused to thaw all day.

He thought she and Rafe were happy, she realised wretchedly. But he didn't know her husband was in love with another woman, that Rafe might not even always be around to share her life. And if he wasn't, what would she tell her son or daughter about her marriage and their father when he or she was old enough to ask? That he had never loved her? That they themselves had been conceived simply out of an act of revenge? Dear heaven! How could she live with the knowledge that one day she might have to tell her child that?

Agony tore a small sound from her lips, and at the same time she heard Myrtle shriek in the back. She looked up, fear paralysing her as Malcolm swung the car violently to try and avoid the articulated lorry that had jackknifed on the icy road. She was aware of a deafening squeal of brakes—of sudden sharp pain tearing though her—and then she seemed to be spinning, round and round, then down and down into nothingness.

CHAPTER NINE

ERICA was floating in a deep, dark chasm. From somewhere way above her, voices drifted down, broken fragments of conversation echoing hollowly in the darkness. They were voices she recognised, one rich and masculine, the other feminine and foreign, yet she was alone, and it was a loneliness that came from a deep, heartrending sense of loss. Then she opened her eyes.

Rafe was sitting beside her, his handsome face—harshened by weary lines—softening a little as he bent over her.

'Thank God! You've had us all worried. Going to speak to me at last, my Erica?'

She frowned, puzzled by the relief she saw in him, until she became aware of the pain in her left shoulder, that she was lying in a hospital bed with a throbbing headache, and that she had been dreaming. But that overwhelming sense of loss was very real, and she looked down at the unfamiliar lines of her body with a sudden, blinding upsurge of emotion.

'My baby...?'

'Now don't go upsetting yourself, Mrs Cameron.' They were the practical tones of a very efficient-looking sister. 'You've been a very fortunate girl, and on top of that you've given your husband a beautiful, healthy little son.'

Relief was overpowering, and she shut her eyes fast against the emotion that welled up in her again, and thought she heard Rafe catch his breath. But then, he'd thought she hadn't wanted it ...

'...did a Caesarean section while you were still comatose,' she recovered to hear the sister enlarging, 'so you got out of doing any of the usual hard work!'

Erica managed a smile at the woman's brusque humour, though her eyes were dark-circled, huge in her small face as she turned them back to Rafe.

'You've had me at my wits' end,' he said hoarsely, and she wondered why he looked so drawn—as if he'd aged ten years overnight. 'When they told me that that car was a write-off...'

The car! She remembered it all now. Myrtle. Malcolm saying how lucky Rafe was. Then the horror of that lorry coming straight towards them...

'Malcolm?' she queried tremulously, her voice urgent, afraid. 'Malcolm and Myrtle...?'

'Both all right. Malcolm sprained his little finger, but your hardy little housekeeper came out of it all without a scratch.' He smiled then, that heart-stopping gesture that broke through the weary cast of his features, ir-radiating the strong lines of the face she loved so much. 'The other driver's a bit shaken, but he didn't suffer any physical harm. It's just you...' Oddly, his voice cracked so that she looked at him wonderingly, unable to identify the emotion in those half-hooded eyes. But with a glance around at the pale, sterile walls, he was saying with a deprecating grimace, 'You're making too much of a habit of this.'

'I'm sorry.' Her mouth curved a little, brightening the gentle angles of her face, and suddenly she became con-scious of the fingers interlocked with hers. She looked down at their hands, at the dark hairs tapering across the back of Rafe's so that it looked strong and pro-tective holding hers. But it was only from natural relief—it wasn't because he loved her, she reminded herself painfully—because hadn't she found that watch engraved with the love he still shared with Vikki? With a spearing anguish, carefully she drew her hand away, incognisant of the shadow that flitted across his face.

'Here we are, Mrs Cameron! I've sent for the doctor to come and look at you. But I don't think it'll do you any harm to make the acquaintance of your son.'

She hadn't even been aware that the sister had left the room, but now the woman was placing the tiny, white-swathed bundle into her arms.

She winced when she moved to cradle her child, but the pain was outweighed by pleasure as she held his warm, little body against her, looking down at the perfect, miniature hands and crumpled face, his little crown of blond hair—almost the same colour as her own—and the deep, ocean-blue of those eyes—Rafe's eyes.

'I think he's hungry,' Rafe informed her, as the tiny face puckered even more, and small, jerky croaks gave way to a surprisingly strong demonstration of lung-power. 'He's been wondering if his mummy was ever going to wake up and feed him, although I think the hospital's probably been dishing him up their own idea of cordon bleu.'

Erica laughed, her hair tumbling forward as she gazed down at the perfect little miracle in her arms. 'When was he born?' The eyes she lifted to Rafe glowed—in spite of everything—with a deep, maternal pride.

'In precisely...' diligently, he consulted his watch '...fourteen minutes and...twenty-nine seconds, he'll be exactly nine hours old.'

'You sound like the speaking clock!' she reproved, unable to hide a smile. It was obvious that, in spite of a lack of any real feeling for her, he was very proud of his son.

The sister had left them again, but a young student nurse had come in, and, seeing Erica sitting up and holding her baby, said brightly, 'Nice to see you awake at last. You look much more like your photograph from a vertical position!' She picked up a newspaper that had been lying on a spare locker, handing it to Erica. 'That's what comes of being Sir Joshua Witney's daughter! You've made front-page news!'

Sure enough, her picture was there, the story beneath it referring to yesterday's accident and the fact that she had been pregnant, going on to report the details of the baby's birth. But the paper made rather a meal of the charges hanging over his grandfather. In fact, the article was worded in such a way that, while not being libellous, seriously questioned the man's innocence, and, recoiling inside, her lips compressing in wounded mutiny, Erica pushed the newspaper aside, looking levelly at Rafe to say, 'Well . . . you've got your baby . . . Will you do something about it now?'

His face was a taut mask, eyes flickering with some unrecognisable emotion, and his hesitancy made her catch her breath. Surely, he couldn't refuse any longer? she thought with tormented reasoning. She had kept to her bargain—paid the debt he thought she owed him in full.

Hurting unbearably inside, she cradled her son protectively against her breast, unable to hide another wince as pain stabbed her left shoulder. 'Well?' she pressed, somewhat shakily now.

His expression was shuttered, eyes strangely guarded as he breathed heavily, 'Yes . . . well, I've been meaning to talk to you about that, but I think it can wait at least until you're out of here.' His eyes appraised her small, strained features. 'Erica . . .' His tone was suddenly low—quieter. 'I think it more important that we talk——'

He broke off as the sister returned with the student nurse and an auxiliary in tow, telling Rafe with a brusque efficiency that the doctor was on his way and that he would have to leave.

'I'll see you later,' he promised, so softly that she wanted to cry, his lips against her hair a gesture that brought him agonisingly close to her, sending her senses into chaos, her heart ricocheting off her ribs. But was it for the benefit of the others?

She watched him go, her attention held by the torturingly dear familiarity of his physique, that arresting male presence that caught the interest of the two younger nurses, too, she noticed, wondering what it was he had wanted to talk to her about. What had he been going to say?

The sound of the door opening intruded upon her somnolent senses. Languorously, Erica stirred, suddenly brought to full consciousness by the sight of the snowy-haired figure who had just come in.

'Erica, my love . . . thank heaven you're all right! I've been imagining the worst ever since Rafe rang me this morning and told me you were unconscious.' Sir Joshua Witncy sat down on the bed, clasping his daughter to him. 'I flew up as soon as I could.'

So Rafe had telephoned him.

'I'm all right, Dad . . . really,' she assured him, suddenly finding her misery almost too much to contain in her father's comforting embrace. But pouring out her heart would have made him unhappy—given him more worry than he already had—she realised, struggling for control as she explained, 'All I've got are a few bruises and a bump on the head, but that one's under my hair so it doesn't show anyway. Things could have been worse—much worse,' she expressed, more composed now. 'But I've been very lucky. We both have...'

As if on cue, a small gurgle came from the cot on the other side of the bed. Sir Joshua craned his neck to see.

'A boy?' he queried, noting the little blue satin bows one of the nurses had tied to the cot. Erica nodded. 'I meant to ask Rafe what it was when he told me the baby was all right,' he admitted, getting to his feet, 'but he sounded so fraught with worry, I didn't like to ask. May I?'

Erica gave another nod, deciding, as her father lifted his grandson out of his cot, that he must have been mistaken about Rafe. He'd been concerned for her, it was true. Extremely so, probably. But fraught? She couldn't imagine that at all.

Ignoring the agony that seemed to be twisting her heart, she looked up at her father holding her son, and with a wan smile said, 'We've decided to call him Adam Joshua—after two very special scientists!'

The man laughed, obviously proud and overjoyed to be a grandparent. In fact he looked remarkably relaxed, Erica noticed, considering all he had been through—was still going through—while he was still on bail. But soon now it would be over, she thought beneath a suffocating emotion, telling herself that, whatever it had cost her to have her father's innocence proved, it had been worth it.

'Rafe's father would have been proud of him—and of the two of you,' Sir Joshua stated, placing his namesake carefully back into his cot. 'You know, he always said he hoped that the pair of you would marry.' Erica didn't say anything. What was there to say?

Glancing away, she noticed the newspaper lying, front page up, on the locker where someone had put it, and as casually as she could she turned it over, hoping that

Sir Joshua hadn't seen. But he had turned round too soon, saying with a grimace, 'I appreciate your trying to hide it from me, love, but I've already seen it. In Reception—when I was waiting to come up. Anyway, it doesn't matter any more, does it? The papers can say what they like. But when we get into court next month that file of Adam's Rafe found will blow Burketts' accusations to smithereens.'

'Then...then he's given it to you...already?' Her heart seemed to stop as she looked up at her father, bewildered, and she saw a furrow appear between his eyes.

'You know he did, sweetheart—months ago. Don't you remember? We were talking about it when you came down last time—on the golf-course. Do you remember that? Coming to stay with me at the New Year?'

Of course, she did, she reflected, worried for a moment, trying to recall what they had talked about during those walks. Witneys, mainly. And the baby. And her father saying something about all his troubles being over because of Rafe. She'd thought he'd been talking about the company, though she could see now how she could have misconstrued what he'd said. And he wouldn't even have needed to mention receiving that evidence from Rafe, thinking that it was obvious—that she had known...

'It's all right—I haven't got amnesia.' She smiled to put his mind at rest. 'I remember everything now.' Even how much brighter he'd looked—how much happier, she reflected—though she'd been too wrapped up in her own problems to give much thought to it at the time.

'Well, the sister told me not to tire you, and you know what a dragon she is!' His buoyancy cut across her whirling thoughts, inducing her to smile again, while she struggled to come to terms with the fact that her husband wasn't quite as mercenary as she'd imagined him to be all along. 'Anyway, Graham volunteered to come with me when I told him what had happened, and I left him downstairs somewhere drinking that putrid excuse for tea. He wouldn't come up. I think he thought it was for the best, but he'll be wanting to know if you're all right, so I'd better go down and ease his mind. You hurry up and get better.' Fondly, she returned his parting hug, while fleetingly considering that Graham must have cared a little more than she'd realised. Then, as her father left, tentatively she eased herself out of bed, going over to the door to peer through the small glass window to watch him go, although he'd turned outside her room so that he was soon out of view.

About to go back to bed, she paused, catching sight of the two people at the end of the corridor immediately parallel with her door. She saw Rafe incline his dark head—say something to the beautiful, raven-haired woman beside him. Then Vikki Stavros reached up and touched his cheek, and he caught her hand, holding it there, a silent, unmistakable communication between two people who shared something very special...

Pain tore through her, and somehow she staggered back to the bed, the discomfort of her bruises—even her feelings in discovering Rafe's consideration for her father—overshadowed by the intense mental anguish she was suffering from what she had seen.

So she hadn't merely dreamt about Vikki. She was working there! Erica acknowledged agonisingly. Because the girl had been in uniform. But that one, simple gesture only served to tell her what she already knew. He loved the Greek girl—he had even let her follow him to Scotland—and nothing, not even giving him a child, had softened him towards her, she realised, a small sob tearing from her lungs. Oh dear heaven! Why couldn't she have had a place in his heart?

She pretended to be asleep when he came in, but couldn't help flinching as he planted a light kiss on her temple.

'Are you asleep, or just pretending?' he breathed against her ear, amused—disconcertingly aware—although his smile faded when he saw the injured look in her eyes. 'What's wrong?' he pressed gently.

What could she tell him? she thought wretchedly, sitting up. 'I've just seen you with the woman you love?' Instead, she said casually, plucking at the coverlet, 'Nothing. Dad was just here.' She faced him then. 'Why didn't you tell me you'd already given him that evidence? Why did you go on letting me think you were holding on to it still?'

He shrugged, his hard mouth firming. 'Maybe because you thought I was cruel enough to do it, though I'm amazed you didn't guess long before now. Did you really think I'd have let him suffer all this time—risk his life?' he quizzed with a hard admonition, so that she glanced away, realising now that it would have been beneath his code of honour to have done something like that. After all, it was only her he had wanted to hurt.

'Caddis was here, too, wasn't he?' Rafe's voice, changing the subject, was flat—toneless—and before she could say anything, he said, 'I know. I saw him talking to someone by the drinks machine downstairs.'

His eyes were dark and searching, but she was too eaten out with misery from that tender scene she had witnessed between him and Vikki to even bother to explain that the other man hadn't actually come up to see her.

She moved, her face twisting as her left shoulder reminded her, in no uncertain terms, of the bruises it had sustained.

'Is this where it hurts?' Rafe's hand was gently cupping her shoulder, and she sucked in her breath, closing her eyes, not so much because it hurt, but because his tenderness was almost too much to bear. Her pulse quickening, she felt her body's simultaneous response to his touch, even though her brain knew—had witnessed—his betrayal. 'You're beautiful.' She could feel his gaze running over the smooth contours of her face, down the silken length of her throat to the rather prim lace of the nightdress the hospital had loaned her, and very gently he pushed back the swathe of blonde hair that fell against his hand. 'This morning when you were lying here with my child in your arms, I thought I'd never seen you look more beautiful... Aurora. My own dawn goddess. You know you could have turned me into anything you wanted—any time—don't you?'

Oh, goodness! Why was he doing this to her? Saying these things? And with a kind of finality that she was too afraid to question.

Almost contrary to her wishes, her lashes fluttered apart, her guarded eyes meeting a naked hunger in his that shocked her, even as she felt her femininity's answering response to it. But then, that sick desire that had held her in thrall whenever he was near had ravaged him, too. It was nothing but a physical attraction that had enslaved him—still enslaved him—even though he was in love with another woman.

'I did a lot of thinking while you were lying here unconscious last night,' he said huskily. 'I've been wrong imagining things could go on the way they have been between us.' He was scanning her delicate features with something in his that resembled pain, those keen eyes not blind to the dark smudges beneath hers—that rather strained look about her caused by more than just her physical injuries—and he inhaled sharply. 'What I'm

trying to say is...' his voice was very controlled, as if
he was picking his words with extreme care '...as soon
as you're well...I've decided it'll be best if I make the
necessary arrangements for you to go home. I'll want
access to my son, of course. You can't expect any less
from me than that. And I'm afraid I won't be satisfied
in just being a weekend father. I'll expect to be involved
in his upbringing—his education—jointly with you. But
apart from that you'll be free of me...to do as you
please...as soon as we can get the...divorce over with.'

She had expected something like this. Nevertheless, it
still came like a swift, cruel blow, so that it took all her
control not to break down in front of him, even though
her heart screamed, I love you! Please don't leave me!

But he didn't need her now. He had the child he'd
wanted from her, plus a good stake in Witneys—which
was the reason he'd married her in the first place, she
reminded herself with bitter anguish—and, of course,
he had his beautiful Vikki, the woman he really loved.
She could only be grateful, as she felt the icy claws of
his cold-bloodedness ripping at her heart, that he had
never fully realised the extent of *her* feeling for
him.

She was packing when the telephone rang. She paused
from folding a sweater, her stomach turning a queasy
somersault as she wondered if it might be Rafe, that—
crazily!—he might be asking her to stay. Which was ridiculous, she thought, self-chidingly, when he loved
someone else, and when he'd treated her with only an
aloof courtesy since she'd left the hospital two weeks
ago. For pity's sake! Where was her pride?

Well, wherever it was, it didn't prevent an irrational
disappointment when she picked up the phone and found
that it wasn't Rafe who answered.

'Erica! How are you? We haven't had a chance to talk yet.' It was only after a few moments that she recognised the heavily accented voice. 'It's Vikki Stavros,' came the announcement, the same second realisation dawned. 'I know I should have spoken to you before, but circumstances prevented it. You're fully recovered, I hope?'

Bemused, Erica murmured that she was—she still had a few fading bruises—but she wondered what Vikki could possibly want to talk to her about. To apologise for taking her husband away from her?

'I was coming off duty when they brought you in,' through her cold, bitter misery Erica heard the girl continue, 'and I decided to come back later and give Rafe some moral support until you regained consciousness. I must have left only minutes before you did, but didn't find out until I bumped into Rafe accidentally later that day. I told him I'd come in and speak to you as soon as I had a minute to spare, but then I decided it wasn't wise.'

'Oh?' Erica couldn't keep the chill out of her voice. Had Vikki's conscience then ultimately persuaded her that the time wasn't right to tell someone she was in love with her husband, after they'd spent all night concussed and giving birth? She had to stifle a sob.

'I was starting a fever and aching all over—that's why I didn't come in to see you again. Just imagine! One week in Scotland in a new job, and then away for the next three with flu! Matron wasn't very pleased, as you can probably guess. By the way... has Rafe mentioned...' there was unmistakable hesitancy in Vikki's voice '...said anything to you...about the watch I gave him?'

Erica stared at the receiver, her forehead wrinkling in anger and disbelief. How did Vikki have the nerve...? This girl really was too much!

'No, he hasn't!' she uttered quickly, with more vitriol than she had intended, because she certainly had no intention of giving Vikki the satisfaction of knowing she had seen the expensive and very personal gift the woman had given her husband.

'Oh, hell.' Clearly, Vikki thought she had put her foot in it, Erica realised, nursing a cold, sick pleasure at the other girl's embarrassment. If Vikki *could* be embarrassed, she thought hatefully. She sounded almost as though she wished Erica had known. Which Vikki did, she realised, shocked, when the woman enlarged hurtfully, with a total lack of compunction, 'You see, he was with me when I bought it—the weekend I came up to Dundee to look for a flat.' She didn't want to know this! Erica inhaled sharply, unable to speak for the pain that seemed to be burning like a red-hot poker through her heart. 'I had it engraved—then found it wasn't working properly,' Vikki went on blatantly. 'Rafe said he'd take it back to the jeweller's as I was still in London at the time and couldn't get there, so when he was down in Cam's head office at the New Year I took it in to him, but he wasn't there. I put a note in the bag and left it on his desk, and I wanted to know if he'd managed to get it repaired as it's Andy's birthday next week.'

Erica's brows drew together. 'Andy?' she echoed into the mouthpiece, thoroughly bewildered.

'My fiancé! Don't tell me Rafe hasn't told you!' came the unbelievable response down the line. 'Andy works with him,' the girl explained, while Erica, suddenly feeling weak, flopped down on to the bed. 'I met him when Rafe first brought the irrigation team to Greece ages ago, but I wasn't that impressed by him then. Who would be—with Rafe around?' she enthused guilelessly. 'But he was persistent—writing to me, flying out occasionally—until eventually I fell and then I couldn't bear to see him go. So what could I do but get employment here so that I could be with him all the time? I was living in temporary digs—doing agency work in London at first as I knew that after Christmas Rafe was going to be transferring Andy to Dundee. I told Rafe that now we're settled up here you would both have to come to see us at the flat, but then you had your accident and I became sick...' Erica could almost feel the little shrug of regret at the other end of the line as she tried to assimilate all that Vikki was saying.

So Rafe wasn't having an affair with the Greek girl— and Vikki was going to marry someone else. The relief was almost unbearable so that she wanted to laugh—to cry! She wasn't quite sure which. She had totally mis-interpreted the meaning of that watch, she realised, be-rating herself, which would also mean then that that intimate gesture she had witnessed in the hospital must have been what...? Simply a token of affection and consolation between...friends? He didn't love Vikki! He didn't! And yet he still wanted her, Erica, to leave...

'...you really must come and meet Andy when you can.' She dragged her concentration back to the tele-phone to catch Vikki's warm invitation. 'I think he's wonderful, but then he has to be to measure up to the man I thought I'd found in Rafe. You're very lucky,' she expressed, sending a small dart of pain through Erica. 'He only ever saw me as a small sister—just a friend. But you...' Vikki's voice held an amiable note of envy. 'That night I kept him company at your bedside, I took a couple of hours off to get some sleep and suggested he did the same, but I don't think he left that chair all night. He didn't say much about how he felt—he never has been one for showing his feelings—but I guessed he was very—what's the word...distraught?'

Erica couldn't come to terms with all she was hearing. Vikki had to be mistaken, she thought. Perhaps it was merely guilt that had kept him at her bedside, guilt from forcing her to marry him in the way he had. A lump came into her throat while she checked the tears that were too near the surface. But feeling bad about the way she had totally misjudged the other girl, she said genially, 'Thank you for being there, Vikki.'

The young nurse seemed quite touched, Erica thought, when she had replaced the receiver, and, going over to stand by the window, considered what Vikki had said about Rafe's being distraught. If that were true, it would mean that he cared. But he didn't, she assured herself with agonising acceptance, otherwise why hadn't he tried to dissuade her when she had quietly accepted his arrangements for her and Adam to go home? Strangely, though, Sir Joshua, too, had said something along the same lines...

Her gaze scanned the wintry scene outside, and was held by a redwing that was tugging ravenously at the orange berries of the fire-thorn bush Rafe had planted for her last autumn. She shut her mind against the memory—the thought of his lovemaking—his tenderness towards her that afternoon—too agonising to bear. Instead, she forced her attention to stay on the hungry bird. Its russet flanks were quite striking against the light fall of snow they had had that day, and absently she smiled, recalling her first sighting of a redwing.

It had been in her school grounds when she was a child, and no one had believed her when she said she'd seen a thrush with a robin's colouring; even the teacher, with her smiling adult scepticism, had made her doubt herself, wonder if she hadn't just imagined what she had seen. It wasn't until one winter morning, years later, when, to her surprise, she'd spotted a flock of them sporting their bright plumages in the tree at the end of her father's lawn, that she realised she hadn't imagined that original bird at all—that her own observations, however juvenile and lightly brushed aside as fanciful all those years before, had been right all along. So couldn't that same doubting part of herself have made a similar mistake about Rafe now?

The thought struck her—jolting her out of her reverie. She remembered the way she caught him looking at her sometimes when she glanced up unexpectedly—eyes dark and brooding—how he always turned swiftly away. Then there were those times when she felt something emanating from him, so tangible, she could bask in its warmth, before that hard mask came down over his features like a solid, cold wall of impregnability. Perhaps, then, what she had often dismissed as mere figments of her imagination were really...

She drew up her thoughts quickly. Could it be possible? Was it even imaginable for one moment that Rafe could be in love with her again? Had he ever really stopped loving her? she wondered with a surge of debilitating hope. Was it even possible he could have felt that way when he'd given her that ultimatum about marrying him?

But no, a little inner voice tried to dissuade her from thinking. That wasn't the way a man in love behaved. Also, if he loved her, why was he letting her go now so calmly, without even trying to stop her? Deep down, though, she knew the answer to that. Rafe was too proud a man to humble himself to any woman, especially when he believed her to be in love with someone else. And all along, of course, she had let him think there was Graham Caddis...

Her heart thudding, she crossed purposefully back to the bed. Later she might regret this, she thought, tingling with nervous apprehension as she closed her suitcase, but she was in love—desperately—perhaps even hopelessly. But if Rafe felt the same way, then she had to know, and there was only one way to find out.

CHAPTER TEN

ERICA looked in on Adam and found him sleeping peacefully before coming downstairs.

As usual, Myrtle had prepared dinner, after which Erica had persuaded her to take the evening off—albeit with some difficulty, she thought, with a grimace—as Myrtle had been rather insistent about helping her to pack. As far as the housekeeper was concerned, she was leaving tomorrow to spend some time with her father although Erica hadn't yet been able to bring herself to tell the other woman that, if she left with Adam tomorrow, she would never be coming back.

Now, as she came into the lounge with its cheerfully crackling fire, she experienced a bout of the nerves she had felt earlier that afternoon, and again wondered if she wouldn't find herself at the end of the evening regretting her reckless decision.

She tensed, hearing Rafe's car coming up the drive, then a few minutes later the front door opening.

'Hello, Erica. I...' Words seemed to fail him as he came into the room, his body stiffening beneath the dark suit, surprise crossing his face. It was the first time she had taken care to dress for dinner since Adam was born, often too tired after the daily schedule of nappy changing, feeding and generally nursing her little son. But tonight she had substituted her usual leisure-suits for a snug-fitting, royal-blue dress. Its simple design and soft material enhanced every curve of her newly regained figure, and she had donned a pair of flatteringly sheer stockings to go with her blue, high-heeled shoes.

She had used more than a modest amount of make-up and washed her hair as well, finger-drying it under the hairdrier so that when she had thrown back her head the blonde strands had fallen about her shoulders in a frenzy of wild silk, which, with her heavily shaded eyelids and dark, creamy mouth, lent her a rather abandoned look.

'Well,' Rafe began, oddly breathless. 'What's all this in aid of?' He seemed annoyed, as well as to be finding some difficulty taking his eyes off her as he crossed the room, tossing his executive case down on to the settee. 'Is this one last attempt to reassure yourself of how desirable I find you before you go?'

His hands seemed remarkably steady as he poured himself a Bacardi and orange juice from the cabinet in the recess—as steady as hers were trembling—and it took all the courage she had to say levelly, 'Well, don't you?'

Her heart was a debilitating thud against her ribs as his head swivelled sharply round. 'What are you trying to do, Erica? See if those feminine wiles still work on me? Because you'd better know now—my resistance level is very low. Push me too far, my sweet, and I won't be able to stop myself even if you beg me to, and I think we might both well end up regretting it in the morning.'

She watched him take a large draught of his Bacardi. His hair curled, thick and dark, against the collar of his shirt, and she felt her stomach churn with longing as her gaze followed the strong, arresting lines of his profile. Supposing she was wrong? she thought, with a sudden pang of misgiving—agony wrenching at her heart. Supposing physical gratification was all he had ever wanted from her? Her entire future happiness—or her total humiliation—could rest on his reactions now.

'Why should *I* regret it?' She couldn't stop her voice faltering as she lifted her small chin in a parody of detachment. 'After all . . . it would be *your* surrender . . . as well as mine.'

Was that pain darkening those narrowing blue eyes—or anger she wondered, feeling queasy. It was impossible to tell.

'Granted,' he conceded, his long fingers appearing to tighten around his glass. 'But with one difference. You have a potential lover waiting in the wings. I make no such claim. What is it you're hoping for in my capitulation to that glorious femininity, Erica? Revenge? Does the need to enslave me one last time outweigh your undying devotion for Caddis? Or are love and sex still so divisible with you that you can walk out of my bed and into his without turning a hair?'

He was angry, and not surprisingly, she thought shuddering, realising just how indiscriminate she must appear to be to him.

He had put his glass down, hands thrust deep into his pockets, his eyes so hard and censuring that Erica tensed, wanting to back down. She wasn't tough enough emotionally to go through with this if she had been wrong about him, yet she knew she had gone too far to pull out now.

She licked suddenly dry lips, realising how provocative the gesture was when Rafe's gaze burned across them, and breathlessly she murmured, 'Who said Graham was ever a candidate?' Heart hammering, she willed her jellied legs to carry her across the space that separated them, and with dizzying courage let her trembling hands slide up over the silk that covered his chest beneath his jacket. She felt him tense, the warmth of him through the fine material with the raw, animal scent of him making her senses swim. He had never looked so hard, so unapproachable, and so unutterably male, she thought giddily, suddenly sharply alive to the thunderous beat of his heart. 'Who said I'm going to Graham after I leave here tomorrow? That's only ever been *your* assumption, Rafe.'

His hands suddenly clamped painfully on to her wrists, and under her helpless fingers his heart increased its heavy rhythm.

'You mean you aren't...? All along you...? Why didn't you tell me?' he rasped throatily, and the tremor that shook his powerful body seemed to shake hers, too. His eyes looked like dark, tumultuous pools as she lifted her face to his, her cheeks pale beneath the stark lines of blusher, every slender feature taut with the anguished words her heart was crying out: I've told you the truth now! Meet me halfway! Tell me you love me! But his lashes only came down to conceal that mysterious emotion in him, although he seemed to need a breath before saying in a voice tight with restraint, 'So what had you in mind? One final fling and then it's over? Well, why not?' he agreed, scathingly hoarse. 'We only ever spoke the same language in bed. And if you want my unconditional surrender, Erica, then you have it, but, so help me I'm going to see that it's one you'll never forget!'

'No!' Her small, pummelling fists were rendered futile as he swept her up in his arms, her stricken cries only curtailed by the thought of what Myrtle would think if she heard them from her room, her heart aching with regret.

He didn't love her! On the strength of her foolish hopes she had gambled and lost, and now she would have to face the pain and degradation of the consequences. But it wasn't pain and degradation—not at first—because these moments, she knew, were all she would ever have with him, and somewhere between the lounge and the bedroom she had stopped fighting him, the demands of her body responding eagerly to the hard, angry urgency of his.

They made love like condemned lovers, each knowing this time would be the last, mouth meeting mouth, flesh meeting flesh in a desperate frenzy of passion that burned all rational thought to dust, the climax when it came a mind-blowing culmination of feelings and sensation that was as immeasurable and timeless as the universe—a transient, dazzling attainment of an unsurmountable joy that gradually faded away, dying like the applause after the final curtain.

It was still dark when she awoke. She'd thought it was morning, but, of course, it couldn't be anything near that, she realised, struggling to see the clock, because Adam would have disturbed her long before now for his regular feed.

So it was over, she thought torturedly, hearing Rafe's steady breathing beside her. She'd be taking her son and going back to London in the morning, and no one, least of all Rafe, would ever know how much it had cost her emotionally.

Trying not to think, she slid out of bed, shivering because he had brought her to his own room earlier, and she had no robe to put on.

'If you're not going to Graham...why are you leaving?'

She had thought he was asleep, the ragged words cutting through her as a restraining hand caught hers.

'Rafe, don't.' It was a small plea.

'Why, Erica?'

'You know why.' Defeatedly, she dropped down on to the bed, shivering again, and almost instantly felt the rough towelling of his robe around her. 'Why did you marry me, Rafe?' she murmured with a small sob, trembling from his touch. 'Was it really only to have a controlling share in the company? Did you really want to hurt me that much?'

'Yes,' he breathed deeply, through gritted teeth, his admission cutting her to the core. He leaned forward, snapping on the lamp, and she blinked, her eyes adjusting, searching his face, hers anguished and strained. He looked tired, she thought through her abject misery, the strong jaw and cheekbones taut as if he was fighting some deep and very private emotion. 'Yes, I wanted to hurt you,' he reiterated, raggedly. 'And if you want to know why—bring me to my knees completely, totally— it was because I was crazy for you, Erica.'

She twisted round in his grasp, trying to make sense of his words, and she saw a bitter smile touch his lips. 'You always were like some half-demented obsession with me, but then you knew that, didn't you?' He exhaled a shuddering sigh. 'So yes, I wanted to put you through what you'd put me through—make you suffer the way I suffered when you told Laverne I wasn't good enough for you and——'

'But I didn't...' Her words tailed away as she strove to comprehend what he was saying, as things suddenly started to become very clear. 'You've always accused me of that, but I didn't know it was because Laverne had said anything...'

'Not only Laverne. You conveyed the message clearly enough yourself when I asked you to marry me. Remember?'

'But I...' Suddenly, she knew that it was time to tell him the truth. He was being frank with her, even if it was hurting her to know the truth. There was no more room for deception now. 'I didn't marry you because...because I knew you wanted children. You made *that* clear to me, but I'd had that operation the year before, and they told me I'd probably never be able to have any. I knew you wouldn't want to marry me if you knew the truth. In fact, apart from Dad, Laverne was the only person who knew. I tried to talk it over with her when you started pressuring me to give you an answer—ask her advice——'

She broke off, choked by the realisation of just how her stepmother had betrayed her trust—using it against her—and she saw comprehension leap into Rafe's eyes, too, flinching from the angry expletive that escaped him.

'Laverne! So she capitalised on your dilemma and put the cat among the pigeons purely for her own selfish ends. Hell! She must have been jealous of you!' he ground out angrily. 'Probably because you were so close to your father and she didn't like taking second place. So she tried to ruin things for you—for us!' His raw anger seemed to shudder through the bare, bronze chest. 'Just because she was jealous—as well as being too highly sexed for a man twenty-five years older than she was!'

'And so because of what she said you made me marry you to get even,' Erica uttered tremulously, her face mirroring the pain she felt inside. 'To have your baby thinking it was the last thing I wanted...'

'No...' a strangely self-deprecating smile curved his lips '...though I might have been angry enough to want you to believe that at the time. I insisted on a child immediately because I believed it would keep you with me long enough for you to change your mind about me. I wanted to make you pay, but at the same time I wanted *you*, so much...'

That deep voice trembled and she looked at him questioningly, aching to touch him, to soothe away the deep grooves that etched his eyes and mouth and made those strong features look oddly vulnerable, but she held back. He'd used words like craving and obsession, and she needed to mean something more to him than that.

'When I thought you were going to lose our baby—that you might not be able to have any more—I thought I'd ruined your life, that it was a punishment to me for forcing you to marry me. I couldn't believe that you'd been too afraid to tell me the truth—that you could honestly have imagined I would have refused to clear your father's name simply because you thought you couldn't provide me with any children. And the only reason I let you think it mattered—kept from telling you that I'd already handed over the evidence—was because I was so annoyed that your opinion of me could be so low. Why the hell did you think I asked you to marry me in the first place—six years ago?' he thrust at her, his tone half incredulous, admonishing. 'Because I wanted *you*, Erica—for yourself—not just for the offspring you'd be likely to provide me with. Of course I wanted children—but that was a secondary factor. Primarily, what I wanted was for you to be my wife. Anyway,' he continued, that strong face shadowed with emotion, 'when you didn't lose the baby, I felt as if I'd been acquitted—that somehow, something was giving us a second chance. I was determined not to take any risks that could jeopardise that possible chance for us—maybe your only chance of motherhood—not to mention protecting our child. Heaven only knows how I managed to stop myself! Sometimes I thought I'd go mad—wanting you so much. Loving you...'

A deep warmth was surging through Erica's veins, and her eyes were sparkling with the incredulous realisation of what he had just said.

'When I did make love to you again, you cried, and I didn't realise then that it was because you simply didn't want to be with me. I thought you were crying because of Graham...'

The harsh light from the lamp emphasised the dark smudges beneath his eyes, so that he looked older, suffering some deep inner anguish that sent a spasm of pain through her heart. But, of course, he didn't know.

'The reason I cried was because I was so happy!' she proclaimed truthfully, and, as if to strengthen her declaration, the hot tears that had welled up inside her cascaded down her cheeks.

'Oh, good grief...' His voice was rough as he caught her against him. 'Why didn't you tell me?' he groaned.

'I couldn't,' she murmured, inhaling the familiar, musky scent of him, welcoming the coarse rasp of his body hair against her softness. 'I didn't know you loved me...'

'Good heavens, Erica! Surely you could tell?'

'Well, no... I mean, I thought——'

'You thought what?' he demanded, brows knitting as he held her away from him.

'I thought... that you and Vikki...'

'Vikki?' He laughed, still frowning, his teeth strong and white against his olive skin. 'Well, I know you were jealous of her, my sweet, but I didn't realise you'd become that paranoid about it. Whatever made you think that?'

She couldn't tell him about the watch, not wanting him to realise just how paranoid she really had been, and she shrugged. 'Oh, I don't know. She was always so pushy. It stood out a mile that she fancied you. And then that morning... after the party... Myrtle said she rang and you drove straight off... like a bat out of hell was the expression I think she used. Why did you?' she ventured tentatively, still a little afraid that her original suspicions might not have been entirely unfounded even now.

A lazy, almost admonitory smile curved Rafe's mouth. 'That was the morning of the conference,' he stated, remembering aloud. 'Andy was already in Norfolk as our computer specialist, setting up the program for the day's talks, which was why he wasn't with Vikki the night before. That morning the whole system crashed out and half the disks were corrupt. Consequently, he rang Vikki in a panic, and she rang me, asking if I could get a set of back-up disks out to him as soon as possible. I shot off to the office—not to see her,' he elucidated with a suggestion of amusement in the deep voice. 'For heaven's sake, Erica, what must I do to prove to you exactly what you mean to me? To make you stay—care—just a little——'

He broke off, his voice cracking, and tightly she wound her arms around his neck, revelling in the knowledge that this strong, self-sufficient man should feel such a depth of emotion for her—such despair—until finally she said, putting him out of his misery, 'Just keep saying it. And I do love you,' she whispered against his rough, male cheek. 'I've always loved you. And I think deep down I half sensed how you felt on countless occasions, but I don't think I really wanted to let myself believe it. It wasn't until Dad told me what . . . what you sounded like when I had that accident . . . and then something Vikki said on the phone . . .'

'Vikki?' he queried, curious, but her heart was too full to explain then, because of the things he had said, her own emotions, and because of the sudden realisation that her child—their child—hadn't been conceived out of vengeance, but was the result of a pure and mutual act of love. 'When I came off the phone, I started thinking about it,' she murmured, as if he'd followed the train her thoughts had taken. 'I decided to seduce you to try and get you to admit you loved me, but you just got angry with me instead.'

'Only because I'd always held back all the feeling I wanted to show you because I thought you hated me. That you were really in love with another man, and all the time...' His tone promised to exact some delicious payment from her for misleading him. 'It worked in the end though, didn't it?' he murmured, his voice, headily seductive, sending a sharp little *frisson* through her.

'I'm not sure. Perhaps I'd better try it again,' she teased, and, slipping back against the pillows, felt the familiar tingling in her body, the stirring of new desire as she saw the answering hunger in Rafe's eyes.

'I love you, dawn goddess,' he whispered, letting her know that he needed no persuasion to express it now, and gently he kissed the pale gold strands at her temples, her closed eyelids, the soft, smooth curve of her cheek. 'I love you, and I intend to start proving it right now.'

'You'll find I take a lot of convincing,' she said mischievously, arching her body readily in wanton abandon to his.

He murmured his approval against her mouth, then gave a frustrated groan at the sudden, untimely reminder from the next room that his small son needed Erica's attention, too.

She giggled at his slow willingness to let her go. 'Don't worry. I'll just have to give you a life sentence,' she promised, smiling wickedly as she sat up to pull on his robe.

'I'll look forward to it,' he grinned. Then, with heartfelt satisfaction, 'We've got so much, haven't we?' he breathed above the strengthening demands of their healthy, hungry little boy. And when Erica nodded in smiling agreement, tenderly he drew her back to him to say, 'I've been a fool. A blind, stupid fool. But at least you had the courage to force me into seeing just what I was losing in not letting you know how much I cared. Thank heavens!' A puzzling line knit the black brows. 'Or should that be Vikki?' he quizzed, half amused.

Of course, he didn't know what the other girl had told her, and for now she decided to keep it locked securely in her heart. She smiled up at him, reaching to touch his cheek lovingly with the back of her hand.

'No, thank the redwing,' she murmured, laughing as she wriggled away.

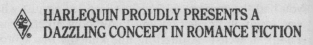

HARLEQUIN PROUDLY PRESENTS A DAZZLING CONCEPT IN ROMANCE FICTION

One small town,
twelve terrific love stories

JOIN US FOR A YEAR IN THE FUTURE OF TYLER

Each book set in Tyler is a self-contained love story; together, the twelve novels stitch the fabric of the community.

LOSE YOUR HEART TO TYLER!

Join us for the second TYLER book, BRIGHT HOPES, by Pat Warren, available in April.

Former Olympic track star Pam Casals arrives in Tyler to coach the high school team. Phys ed instructor Patrick Kelsey is first resentful, then delighted. And rumors fly about the dead body discovered at the lodge.

Following the success of WITH THIS RING,
Harlequin cordially invites you to enjoy the
romance of the wedding season with

BARBARA BRETTON
RITA CLAY ESTRADA
SANDRA JAMES
DEBBIE MACOMBER

A collection of romantic stories that celebrate the joy,
excitement, and mishaps of planning that special day
by these four award-winning Harlequin authors.

**Available in April at your favorite Harlequin
retail outlets.**

Janet Dailey®

Americana

Janet Dailey's perennially popular Americana series
continues with more exciting states!

Don't miss this romantic tour of America through
fifty favorite Harlequin Presents novels, each one set
in a different state, and researched by Janet and her
husband, Bill.

A journey of a lifetime in one cherished collection.

April titles   **#29 NEW HAMPSHIRE**
              Heart of Stone

              #30 NEW JERSEY
              One of the Boys

Jackson: Honesty was his policy...
and the price he demanded of the woman
he loved.

THE LAST HONEST MAN
by Leandra Logan
Temptation #393, May 1992

All men are not created equal. Some are
rough around the edges. Tough-minded but
tenderhearted. Incredibly sexy. The tempting
fulfillment of every woman's fantasy.

When it's time to fight for what they believe in,
to win that special woman, our Rebels and Rogues
are heroes at heart. Twelve Rebels and Rogues,
one each month in 1992, only from
Harlequin Temptation!